WELCOME TO THE WORLD OF HOUSE SECRETS

This book takes place at the same time as *Blood Secrets* "The Sorcerer's Touch." There exists a parallel between that story and As Dawn Breaks, as House Secrets is a *continuation* of the Blood Secrets trilogy, so I have not included details Attar's battle as that is part of the Blood Secrets storyline.

While the book ***can*** be read on its own, there are concepts and people in the Blood Secrets series which clarify some of the action in this story. It is recommended that you read those books first. However, I will include a brief introduction to the world, explain who is who on the introduction pages following and include a glossary of commonly used terms.

HOUSE SECRETS

how many secrets are hidden from view?

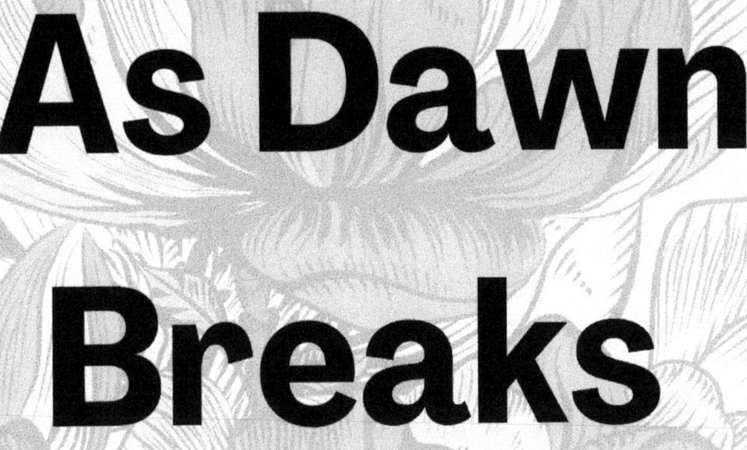

House Secrets
Book One

Imogene Nix

All people, institutions and places in this book are entirely fictional. Any resemblance to actual persons living or dead is entirely coincidental.

Paperback ISBN 978-1-922369-28-4

Ebook ISBN 978-1-922369-27-7

Edited by: Hot Tree Editing

Cover by: Dexpress Covers

Please note:

The UK and USA share the English language, but there are many words that are spelled differently. Some words have extra letters in the British spelling, such as the word cancelled. In American English, it is spelled canceled. There also words that interchange the letters c or s and sometimes z. For example, in America, you spell offense and in Britain, it is written as offence.

These spellings are **not** incorrect.

This book is written in UK English to reflect my Australian/English background.

INTRODUCTION

As the continuation of the Blood Secrets trilogy, some readers may come into the series, unknowing of what has gone before. This is a brief overview of The Blood Bride, The Illuminated Witch and The Sorcerer's Touch to assist you to understand the world you are entering.

In ***The Blood Bride*** we meet Hope, daughter of the House and Xavier, the Vampire Master of the House of Tudor. He's old and she's very young, returning to a divided house where her father holds the title of *Yeux Secondes*. Her brother, David and parents are hostile, but neither quite as much as Alexa—David's wife.

We learn about a secret in Hope's blood which makes her a valuable asset and on more than one occasion the bad guys try to abduct her.

On returning from College she meets Xavier and is fascinated, but so is he. After an attack she is taken below stairs, into the vampire accomodation for safety and one thing leads to another and Xavier and Hope fall in love.

After an attack, Xavier is injured and she ends up feeding him and she becomes a vampire when things go a little far. She learns to stand on her own two feet and is now a formidable figure, just as we learn about the Alpha Vamp — Attar.

In ***The Illuminated Witch***, we first meet Celina, our witchling orphan, except she doesn't know she's a witch. When illness strikes her down in front of the House of Tudor office building, she meets Javed, second vampire of the house, who will soon be invested with his own nest.

Her magic is swelling and dangerous and she needs assistance, the kind that comes with training. But along the way, there is danger.

As with Hope, she too falls for the Master of this new house but things aren't straight forward. She's abducted and when Javed finds her, she's close to death. He turns her but not before they also finds three children among the many abductees. When Celina and Javed finally reunite as Vampires, they decide they will adopt the three girls—Lucy, Rachel and Marian. Though they aren't actually blood siblings, they've survived together for years and don't want to be split up.

In ***The Sorcerer's Touch***, Daniel joins Hope and Celina in making the choice to turn. He's fallen for Mistress Vampire Cressida and is willing to give up everything for honour, duty and ultimately love.

Cressida and Hope end up adopting orphan nestling, Samantha as their daughter after an attack on another nest.

Together Hope and Xavier, Celina and Javed and Daniel and Cressida must fight the Alpha Vampire Attar, just as was foretold by the three women who are related to Attar, and turn up in all three books—Jemima, Daniella and Danicka.

BLOOD
SECRETS

what secrets are hidden in the blood?

GLOSSARY OF TERMS

Consort The unofficial partner of a Master or Mistress

House The formal name for a nest - eg *The House of Tudor*

Life Partner The official partner of a Master of Mistress

Lycans Weres of any variety

Master The male head of a House

Mistress The female head of a House

Nest A formal title for a house of vampires

Nestling One who chooses to live within a vampire nest

Second The vampiric second of the Master/Mistress of a house.

Yeux Secondes The title bestowed on the human head of a house. Meaning 'second eyes' and equivalent to the Second.

Why not subscribe to

Imogene **Nix's** newsletter?

http://bit.ly/INixNews

PROLOGUE

"Do you know anything about...?" David waved his arm, and Daniel shook his head.

David clamped his arm on his shoulder and squeezed. He knew he was pale, but the reality of the situation impinged.

Hope had glanced at him, smiled tremulously, but didn't approach.

"Are you okay?" Daniel's question swam through David's brain.

He cleared his throat, considered the man before him. "I don't... I'm resigning my commission and plan to seek a place in a new house." The words erupted from him, but once out, David relaxed.

Daniel frowned. "Today?"

He shook his head. "No. When the mess with Attar is done. I've hung in only because... It was Hope who kept me together once I came to terms with what had been done. I treated her badly and so did my parents, and I feel dirty because I believed everything I was told. Now it's hard to stay after..." David shrugged.

"But if Hope forgives you, surely the situation can be resolved?"

"No, Daniel. Everyone knows what I did. What *we* did. How we took her—Alexa's—side and left Hope to suffer the consequences of the lies. It just... it doesn't feel right, you know? She's built something good and true. I can't muddy it any longer than necessary. She needs to rebuild her life free of that taint."

Daniel frowned. "If you need to move, you would be more than welcome with me. I can talk to Javed..."

"No. But thank you." David shook his head. "When it's done... Once Attar is defeated, I'm thinking of going somewhere else."

Sucking in a deep breath, he stepped back around Daniel and wandered to the other side of the room.

Several Months Later

David looked down at his hands. Instead of the neatly manicured nails he'd always sported, ragged edges betrayed the rage he'd held at bay over the last several months.

Now this. The parchment paper in his grip crackled, and he released the hold slightly, forcing himself to read the front page.

Referring to the decree made in this cause... the marriage between the aforementioned Plaintiff and Defendant be dissolved unless sufficient cause be shown to the court...

He wasn't unhappy with the outcome. Neither was he ecstatic. It wasn't the way he'd planned for his life to proceed.

Alexa had lied to him. Made a dupe of him. There'd been no child, and she'd blinded him to truths he should have noted. The betrayal ran deep. She'd colluded with his father, alienated his mother, and damaged the relationship he had with his sister.

The situation felt untenable, really.

But still... The life he'd planned to make was over. Deleted with the stroke of a pen by a Family Court judge.

Slumping back into his chair, David surveyed the room. It was new, pale-coloured walls in a strange boxlike building, yet there was a charm to it. The kind he hadn't ever felt in the old-world manor where he'd grown to adulthood.

He sighed.

Dawn had passed some three hours before, and while he, along with his master, Javed, had agreed the house didn't require an external office set-up at this point, it felt odd to be ordering a coffee and still wearing the lounging pants he'd tugged on after showering at nine in the morning.

The phone buzzed and broke the internal ruminations that occupied his mind.

He answered with a curt "David."

"Sir, we have an officer of the law here. They say it's important they speak with you. Something to do with a situation with the vampires."

"Fine. Give me a moment, then send him in."

"Her, sir."

He blinked. "Of course."

Letting go of the button, he rose from his chair, straightened his clothing—the teachings of his mother still held tight—before lowering himself into the chair, preparing for whatever came to pass.

The door opened, and a slim, dark-haired woman entered the room. She wasn't tall, and her features were regular. Her hair, tied into a neat and tidy braid, was dark brown, though her eyes were a golden green colour.

The impressive creases, carefully aligned in her uniform, and the shine of her shoes told him she was either a new officer or one of those committed to her job. He had a feeling it was the second option.

"David Jardin?"

He inclined his head, and the woman stood, facing him.

Discomfort flowed. In his world, you asked women to sit; they were coddled and kept at home until they married. This woman might look soft, but he noted a spark of something in her eyes and the ramrod straightness of her spine. This was no meek and biddable woman here. It was perverse, but he didn't offer the seat.

"You wanted to talk to me about the vampire attacks?"

She blinked. "Uh, yes. I wanted to make some further enquiries. My name's Officer Fernly, from the Liaison Division, and I need to check some facts to determine—"

His brow furrowed as he concentrated on what had taken place the evening before. He'd found a briefing paper on his desk when he'd entered that morning.

"Oh yes," he interrupted. Something about this woman put him on guard.

She flipped open the tiny notepad she carried. "We have reports of a man attacked by what he believes was a vampire. He escaped, but it terrified him. He's lost a lot of blood and may very well require assistance coming to terms with the attack."

"And what do you want me to do for you today, Officer Fernly?"

"It's been suggested that it's more than just a single attack. We haven't been informed of such a circumstance, and if there's a likelihood of danger to the public—"

He raised a hand. "I'm limited on what I can divulge, Officer." Now he indicated to a seat and watched as she slowly lowered herself to the padded cushion. The closing of her eyes and the gentle exhalation betrayed her emotional state.

"You were on duty last night and attended this call. Yet you're on duty this morning."

The woman seated opposite him glanced in his direction. "I work the hours necessary to get the job done."

Pompous git! He sat there looking terribly comfortable while her body twinged and ached. She'd be damned if she'd rub anything that hurt, though. She'd learned the hard and bitter lesson of never revealing a weakness over the years.

"Liaison Division don't work usual hours. We understand the necessity to interact with all species and the times they inhabit." Inhaling deeply, Genny marshalled her thoughts. He might not respond so well, but there were questions that had to be asked. Answers only a nest member could give.

His mouth flattened at her blunt explanation, and a tiny seed of victory took root. Genny ruthlessly beat it back. No benefit in taking the situation cheap. Or antagonising this *Yeux Secondes*. "What can you tell me about the situation, Mr Jardin?"

"As I said, I am limited in what I may disclose. We're concerned that there's a vampire or vampires roaming the streets and attacking those who can't protect themselves. They've attacked several humans and may pose a security risk to the greater public."

Fury coursed through her. *Security risk?* That didn't explain the gravity of the situation as she'd discovered. Suspicion had also grown that what they'd found in the Liaison Division was merely the tip of the iceberg. "Forgive me, Mr Jardin, but I understand over one hundred have been harmed or killed in the vicinity, without including the loss of vampires. Not to mention attacks on nests internationally. The human population is terrified that they'll be the next targets. We're doing our best to protect them, but in order to do so, we need intelligence. The Liaison Division needs information." On a roll, she didn't hold her tongue. "Information you're withholding."

She watched as the man opposite, darkly good-looking and lean, with a face hewn by the angels themselves, tightened. "As you would be aware, issues with vampires are controlled by the Council and its own, shall we say, police? I believe the information you're demanding is privileged. Officer Fernly, you've overstepped the mark, and I'll ask you to leave."

Rage filled the air. She could almost see it. Taste it. But he was right, she'd demanded something she wasn't entitled to. Her boss would be furious if there was an official sanction lodged, so for now, the best thing she could do was withdraw regretfully.

Even as she mentally gritted her teeth, Genny snapped her notepad shut and smiled. "Forgive me, Mr Jardin. My concern is only for the innocent."

His eyes flashed. "Indeed. However, I have other appointments to attend to."

Well aware she'd been dismissed, Genny stepped forwards, slipped a small pasteboard card onto his desk. "If you feel there's information that would be relevant or we can assist, my details are there."

She left the office, aware of the burning of his gaze on her back.

Genny had felt that before, and on more than one occasion. It had been followed with a blow or attack. She didn't let her guard down until she was outside the house and sliding into the car.

Garrett, her partner, peered at her. "Get what you needed?"

Without a word, Genny turned the key. "No. Let's head back to the station."

He fumed. What did some police officer nobody think she was doing demanding answers he couldn't give? David lurched from his seat and headed for the door. Fresh air might calm some of the jitters that rode him.

But once outside, he was confronted by the preparations that took place around him. Vampires had been housed in secure locations as had nestlings, but some had petitioned for transfers within the nests. The al bin Habbad nest had received forty new nestlings, and while the Council had agreed that such a large number wasn't the best decision when the nest itself was only months old, the needs of the innocent couldn't be understated.

A large bus filled with refugees lumbered up the driveway, and his staff of five had set up tables so they could receive them. One would arrange emergency housing in a complex the Council had closed on just yesterday. He mused at how fast the Council could make things happen.

Like his divorce.

The memory of the paper on his desk soured his gut.

"Jane, has all the furniture been arranged?"

His assistant bit her thumbnail and winced. "I've got most, sir. But there are still some pieces we're trying to find from other suppliers. And there're more children than adults. We've got a list and are arranging fostering, but the kids'll need counselling. We don't have a paed-psych on the books. I've got Ellie making enquiries. Meanwhile, three were injured and will also need medical care. We're going to keep them here for now. Kharisma and her team should have the skills needed."

David nodded and tugged once more at the clothing he wore. "We'd best meet them, then. I want lists, bios, and details on my desk tonight by five." He turned and headed for the bus.

He'd only been partially trained as his father's successor and struggled more than he'd ever expected at the intricacies of the role. The rules to be followed and privileges owed to the nest masters and councillors. Xavier came to mind. He'd only been in the House of Tudor for several months when Hope returned.

Xavier hadn't demanded or pandered. He'd been even-handed with everyone he dealt with. Javed was no different. And Daniel, his cousin who'd been his predecessor here in the new nest, had been personable. Charming and exceptional at the role. It made David's more "stuffy" way of doing things less desirable.

Unsatisfactory.

It was a term he hated with a passion.

He watched as the nestlings filed from the bus. His people would greet them. House them.

David turned away. The office called. With papers to read, decisions to make, and staff to employ, he couldn't afford the time to meet with the weary travellers. That gnawed at him until only one word remained in his mind.

Unsatisfactory.

CHAPTER 1

Genny prowled the townhouse she'd moved into. It wasn't big or luxurious. It wasn't owned by a nest, so the security wasn't as tight as she'd grown up with. But it was hers. Somewhere she could be herself without the concern that anyone would realise what she was.

Dragging the jacket and restrictive uniform shirt off, Genny sighed and flexed aching shoulders.

Her body was still recuperating from the last altercation she'd taken part in. Her chest bore the scars. The ridged lines caught her attention in the mirror, and she traced them. Six long score marks where his nails had dug deep, tearing flesh.

Even now the scent lingered in her memory. Ripe. Coppery.

Her gums ached, and she blinked rapidly, hoping to keep the flash of gold and green in her eyes from flaring.

"Stop it, Genny." It wasn't enough. Her core itched as the beast within demanded release.

One nail elongated, the shimmering pink polish rippling. Genny concentrated and pushed back the urgent demand of the creature. "No. Not tonight."

Soon.

Turning away, Genny headed to the fridge and had only just pulled the door open when her cell pealed. "Genny Fernly."

"Genevieve, *ma petite fille*. You are home, finally." Her mother's voice filled the air, and Genny closed her eyes.

"*Bonjour, Maman*. Yes, I just finished my shift." Her fingers curled around the handle, and the blast of cold air soothed the raging fire that threatened to overcome her.

"You should stop playing with the humans, my dear. You're not one of them."

Genny silently counted to five, trying to avoid the argument that always arose when her mother started down this line. "No I'm not. But I'm doing something useful with my life. I'm in control, and—"

"You should ask Luca Thorne to forgive you, even though it's all his fault, *bebe*. You should be home, raising little—"

"No, *Maman*. I want to be here. I wanted to become an officer, and I'm good at it. No matter that it doesn't meet with your approval, I will continue. I can help those who aren't humans and those who are. If they know and trust us—"

Her mother snorted. "Last time someone tried this, there were pitchforks, *bebe*. You don't remember because you and your brother weren't yet born. They killed and maimed. They will do so again. Living under the radar is the best for us and our kind. *Bah!* I was ringing because your brother has finally found a mate and plans to settle down. You are required to attend the Joining Ceremony."

Genny's gut clenched hard. "A mate? Anyone I know?" How hadn't she known her twin had found someone?

Once, long ago, she'd had hopes. Had met Julien and they'd planned—

Cutting off that train of thought, she shook her head and concentrated on the conversation.

"No, you don't know her because you never come home. Tomorrow evening we're holding a meeting of the clan. You should attend."

Releasing the fridge door, she watched as it clanked shut and then rubbed her finger over her aching brow. "I can't, *Maman*. Send me the details for the Joining and I'll request a day off."

"*Bebe*..."

"I really can't, *Maman*. There're things happening. Bad things, and I need to do my part." Genny tried to inject the urgency into her words, willing her mother to understand. She doubted the woman ever would. Her mother been loyal to the clan, even during the time she'd been banished and nest-placed. That blind fealty had allowed her and her children to return to the clan when the usurper had been removed. But the scars remained, even if they hid in her psyche.

"I have to go. I need to eat and rest. *Je t'aime, Maman*." Pressing the red button to end the call, Genny sighed, reached for the fridge door, and opened it once more. Peering inside, she spied a large piece of steak. Her stomach rumbled as she pulled it from the fridge, taking care to close the door behind her.

Hunger roared, and she closed her eyes. Normally she'd have partly cooked it—a choice she'd practiced until it became close to second nature—but today the craving was bone deep. Genny allowed the incisors in her mouth to elongate and then tore into the flesh, licking her lips to capture the last drips of blood before following up with her fingers.

Turning, she slipped the plate it had rested on into the dishwasher and stood there, glancing out the tiny window that looked out over the city.

Her mother's words echoed in her mind. She wasn't human. She wasn't anything except a hybrid. One who didn't belong anywhere.

Bastien had found a mate. He was fully cat, so the taint didn't revolt others like it did with her. Didn't mark him as unsuitable for mating. The cold in the centre of her belly settled like a weight.

"Learn to live with it, Genny." But as with the millions of times she'd said it before, it didn't make her feel better.

DAVID ALIGHTED FROM THE CAR. THE SUMMONS BY CRESSIDA WAS unwelcome but unsurprising. Daniel met him at the door. Since he'd become Cressida's life mate, he'd grown in confidence and charisma. The red of his irises was still a surprise to David, who'd known the man his entire life. Yet he appeared settled too.

"Daniel. There's a problem?"

Daniel shook his head. "Not exactly. Cressida heard you had a surprise visit from a police officer last night."

David nodded. "Yes, Genevieve Fernly. Uptight and asking questions I'm not at liberty to answer."

Daniel scowled. "Cressida won't be happy to hear that. There was a human some rogue vampire attacked. Not by Attar, but one of those he turned. I doubt they belong to a nest."

"Fernly wanted to know numbers. Details."

The door opened behind him, and he swept a deep obeisance to the woman his cousin had pledged his life to.

"David, please come in. Daniel too."

He followed Cressida, not for the first time wondering how the woman exuded such power yet still appeared young and untouched. They settled into ornate seats, and he waited for Cressida to speak. "You were telling Daniel about a police officer's enquiries. Genevieve Fernly? I'm aware she's wanting to know numbers. I've heard she's driven and wants only the best for the humans and others. The Council has agreed we should bring her into the fold. Not tell her everything, because that would be dangerous, but as much as is safe to divulge. She grew up in a nest, at least for part of her formative years, I've discovered, so she's not unaware of the restrictions."

David nodded his agreement and waited, sure there was more to this meeting than simply talking about what he could disclose to the Liaison Division.

"But I wanted to talk to you about the nest. How you're acclimating."

He groaned inwardly. How did he explain he felt like an ill-fitting jacket? "Things are... fine."

She quirked her brow. "Fine. What an interesting word. What it doesn't do is explain if you feel compromised. Hope, Celina, and Daniel are all vampires, and you're the last of your line, and you've moved into a nest that has—" She coughed and glanced to Daniel, who smiled ruefully. "—a fluid outlook on governance."

David blinked. "I'm sure, with time, I can come to terms with the way Javed sees the nest progressing." He waited. Unless Javed had said something to Cressida? Raised a concern David was unaware of? He'd been taught a *Yeux Secondes* never questioned their leadership. It was a position they came to attain and hold through willpower and hard work.

"I worry that you're feeling discomforted. You were hard to read as a child, and under the mentorship of your father..." Cressida shrugged. "I'm also aware of your personal circumstances. The situation with Alexa has proved fraught, and you've had a lot to come to terms with over the last year or so. We'll support you, David. Not least because you're family."

The words pierced him. *Family*. Could he claim any family these days with the betrayal of his father? The way he'd treated his sister after Alexa had planted seed after poisonous seed in his mind? The knowledge gnawed at him day and night.

"I... Thank you, Councillor." She watched him a moment longer, as if seeking a chink in the armour he gathered around himself. The knowledge that she questioned his state of mind irked him.

"Thank you, David. While you're out, could you deliver Jenna Downton to where she'll be housed?"

He rose and nodded, then was further surprised when she gathered him close and pressed a soft kiss on his cheek. "You're a good man, David. You've just been taught poorly and treated shabbily, but time will give you the opportunity to overcome those things."

He withdrew from the room and headed to the hallway, banishing the myriad of competing emotions. There, waiting for him, stood a young lady of maybe eighteen or nineteen. Her wide green eyes shone in contrast to the pallor of her skin—startlingly bright. Her arm was bandaged, as was her neck.

"Miss Downton?"

She started at his words, and he couldn't mistake the abject fear in her gaze. "Are you... one of *them*?" She shook like a quivering leaf. It tore at him. Was this how most saw vampires—as vicious attackers without a soul? Having grown up in a nest, he knew better.

David shook his head. "Not at all. I'm as human as they come."

She deflated before him. "Where are you taking me?"

"The Council has requested I guide you to the home of a senior nestling. He and his family will look after you while you recuperate, and we attempt to find your family." He reached out a hand, and she took it, the embrace urgent and terrified based on the nails digging deep into the flesh.

She bit her lip and glanced away, but not before he caught sight of the large tears rolling down her face. "They're... dead. The vampires killed them."

"Then we'll help you. Find you somewhere safe to live. The houses will assist." He tugged her towards the door. "Come."

THE EXHAUSTION THAT BATTERED GENNY WAS A CONSTANT. EVEN AS she rubbed her eyes, she knew the truth. Constantly gripping onto the beast inside took its toll. She'd been more than happy to pay and keep paying the price for the domination of her life.

The claw marks reminded her daily that she had to control what lived inside.

A clean uniform and polished boots waited. Her life revolved around the need to serve and protect; whether that was family, friends, or the greater community really didn't matter.

Rising with a grunt, she headed to the bathroom, showering and then ruthlessly taming her hair. Today would be difficult, she knew.

Once dressed, Genny scooped up her keys, fastened her sidearm on her belt, and left the house. A quick drive-through coffee stop and she was ready.

At the precinct, she headed through the secured entrance to the Liaison Division, inhaled deeply. Letting the scents, myriad and strangely calming, wrap themselves around her, she headed for the boss's office. Knocking on the door of his office, she waited until a gruff "Come" echoed.

"Boss?"

"Genevieve. Take a seat." He looked around fifty but, like her, wasn't exactly human. Most of the crew never divulged *exactly* what they were. There was the odd human in the mix, but they were seriously outnumbered. Revealing their true natures was an unspoken need-to-know thing. Just as well, as her other side hadn't ever really manifested.

"I did something last night... uh, this morning, boss. I went to the new vamp nest. The House of al bin Habbad? The vampire attacks aren't all the story, but they are increasing not just in regularity but also the viciousness." Her heart raced madly in her chest, but the boss kept his face passive. It was always disconcerting trying to read his reactions.

"And you pushed too hard. Yes, I'm aware of that, but our victims appear to trust you." He reached for an old-fashioned folder on his desk. Flipped through it while Genny waited. "For what it's worth, I agree with your summation. But tell me, why choose al bin Habbad?" He set the file back on the table.

Genny marshalled her thoughts. "The house is new, and the staffing is iffy. I had more chance of getting in and meeting with the *Yeux Secondes* rather than, say, the House of Tudor."

"Exploit their weakness. Find out what you could. And you learned...?" He steepled his fingers and waited.

"Nothing. David Jardin came from the House of Tudor. He'd been understudy for his father and wasn't as malleable as I'd hoped. I wasn't so cautious with my wording, and he took offense and asked me to leave."

The boss—Belarmino—laughed. "Jardin. They're not really in the best position to throw their weight around after the father was pursued for his actions against the Council. The younger one is in the middle of a divorce too. Yes, I can see how you came to the conclusion." His eyes flashed silver. "Follow it up, Genevieve. Get me the intelligence, because something's about to blow. I can feel it." He rubbed his left shoulder, just as he always did when making a foretelling comment.

Genny rose from the chair. "Boss?"

"They've made no representations that you should be sanctioned. Go about your business, but be careful next time." His voice boomed, echoing through Genny's mind. Eerie and perturbing in the intensity, there was almost a hint of mental manipulation weaving through her system.

Genny blinked, then nearly fled the office for the lunchroom.

Escaped a bullet there.

It was a common occurrence for the boss to explode. On more than one occasion, an officer had retreated, pale and shaking, from the office across the way. Today, Genny was thankful that wasn't her.

"Got roasted?" A tiny woman, Katya, sat at the table, sipping a cup of tea. Genny was almost sure she was a pixie or something similar. Even more important though, she was a whizz at research. If she didn't know something, she knew someone who did. Or had the contacts to get it themselves.

"Thankfully not too bad. Hey, what do you know about the House of Tudor?"

Katya's eyes grew round. "Big house. Established nearly two hundred years ago. Was Councillor Cressida's until the daughter, Hope, was abducted. Been through upheaval recently since the *Yeux Secondes* was caught lining his own pockets, but reasonably stable even though they've had three masters this century and the son of the house left for al bin Habbad. The daughter is a recent turn to vampire and is the life partner of the master, Xavier."

"Wow, that was strangely encyclopaedic, Katya." Her brain hurt at the information that rolled around in her head.

"There's more, but that's the guts of it." She sipped her tea. "Need anything else?"

Genny shook her head and walked to the counter. A disposable cup already in hand, she fixed her coffee—half strength and white.

DAVID CONSIDERED THE YOUNG WOMAN OPPOSITE HIM. JENNA Downton was terrified by the concept of being touched by a vampire, yet the houses—the very central structures that determined vampires' actions—would now shelter her.

"So, Jenna, where were you when this happened?"

The girl blinked. "In my bedroom. Mama and Daddy had just got home from the theatre. Sara and Lilly had gone to bed, and I'd not long got home from classes, so Lana, the babysitter, was still there."

She twined her hands together, and David wanted to reach out and offer support. His parents' training stopped him short, though.

"Then what?" He kept his voice low and unchallenging.

"I heard the glass of the window. It crashed, and I came out onto the landing. Sara and Lilly were there too. Screams. Terrible—" Jenna gulped audibly. "—awful screams. Then a blur before me. Lilly and Sara." She slid her hands around her body as if trying to hold in her soul. "They went up and down, and blood sprayed. Hot. It washed over me. Sticky. Lana came out of the bathroom and saw. She tried to stop it. I rang the line, you know the one on the television, and then I felt it. He laughed. Eyes red and blood coated him. He grabbed me, hurt me, but I remembered the rules. Hit hard. Aim for the head. I got him, but he ran away."

Jenna sobbed, and David moved forwards against his instincts. Gathered her close and felt the shudders that racked her frame.

The car turned into a driveway. The house was just like any other suburban residence, except David knew the added security included metal shutters, guards, and more than one member who was highly trained in martial arts. Enough to hold off a vampire until help could arrive.

As they drove up to the house, he wondered if perhaps the work of Officer Fernly was in fact necessary for every part of their democratic principles to work. Perhaps they were attacking the Liaison Division situation poorly?

The door opened while he thought, and he released Jenna from his embrace. He reached into his pocket and pulled out a card. "Jenna, here's how to contact me. If you need anything or just want to talk, call me."

Father would be horrified, and Mother would be furious. But they weren't here, and he'd had no contact with them since they'd left the house that day.

"Thank you," she said and took the card before climbing out of the vehicle.

"Thank you, Mr David. We appreciate your assistance." The woman who'd met the car smiled and bobbed a quick curtsey. It was the type of greeting his father would have expected, and he wondered if perhaps that alone was the reason. He felt distaste at the action. But how did he tell them not to do so? Yet another problem to be overcome.

He waited until the women were once more inside before he closed the door. “Markus, would you take me to the warehouse? I’d like to check on the shipment about to go out.” Not that checking in was necessary, but he needed time away from the pressure cooker to consider what had occurred to him.

The trip was slow, as they were caught in the early evening rush hour traffic. Not that it bothered him because it allowed him more time to think over the revelations that continued to bombard him.

Glancing out the window, he saw the lines of traffic. Old cars. New cars. Families with bored-looking drivers. Some gazed back at his vehicle, no doubt seeing the sleek and shiny car and wishing they could step into his life.

“I’d give it to them, right now,” he muttered.

“What’s wrong, Mr David?” Markus called from the front.

“Nothing.” He turned back. “Do you ever wish your life was different?”

He caught the glance of the driver’s eyes in the mirror. Surprise.

“Uh, no. I mean, it would be great to have more money, but I live a good life. I have opportunities to do more, be more. The houses have policies to help those who want their own businesses. One day, I will, but for now? I have a place to live, and it’s secure. Plus I’m paid a good wage.”

David mused on Markus’s words as they drove into the industrial estate where the house processed their wares. It wasn’t big, but they’d bought the largest facility available, allowing for them to expand into the future.

This was where he’d give back to the community that housed him, paid for his education. He’d give them his all.

Straightening his suit, David opened the door and stepped out. He’d only recently taken over from Daniel, yet everywhere he looked, he could see the hallmarks of the man’s touch. The placements of the bathrooms in the work areas and the range of refreshments available to the staff and the new architectural style. Furnishings chosen for comfort over "style" his mother had demanded. Comfortable, casual clothing worn in the house rather than stiff monogrammed shirts, pencil skirts, and pressed slacks his previous house staff had worn uniformly.

"Sir, we've received a shipment this morning, and we're happy to announce our schedule is not just on track but currently two weeks ahead." The woman who sidled up beside him carried a clipboard and wore a scarlet hard hat.

"Serena?" He guessed her name, and she bobbed her head. The fiftyish woman handed him a black hat, which he slipped on. "Could you give me a quick tour? I've been trying to get here all week, but with the fallout from the attacks—"

She nodded, and as they walked through the plant, she pointed out Daniel's improvements. By the end, he was assured that this crew knew better what needed to happen on the manufacturing side than he did. She passed him an envelope with a range of printouts. "I'll look them over this week and get back to you as soon as I can."

He made his way back to the car and checked his watch. Eight o'clock. If he headed back to the house, he'd be able to eat, then retreat upstairs to shower and look over the information in peace.

"Let's go home, Markus," he instructed.

They'd just pulled into traffic when the phone rang.

"David Jardin."

"Alert." He sat up straight, dread coursing through his veins. The automated system continued, "An attack on a nest in New Orleans. It's a total loss, from what we understand. No survivors."

He swore. "Engage flight. Get us back to the house as swiftly as possible," he called to Markus, then reached over, picking up the handset now that the previous call had disconnected. He needed to get the house locked down as swiftly as possible.

The car sped up, then took to the air, the forces pushing him back into his seat with a grunt as he began the preparations.

CHAPTER 2

Genny scrubbed her hands over her face while the computer screen wavered in front of her. "Ugh, this makes no sense."

If only her job was as exciting as some people thought. It wasn't all car chases and quick outcomes. Ninety-nine percent of her job was research, computer work, or pounding pavement. But given it was near to midnight, unless there was something pressing, she wouldn't be leaving the precinct any time soon.

Heading back to the break room, she stopped, hearing a wild commotion. Her legs propelled her forwards as other people gathered around the small television mounted on the wall.

"What's going on?"

Her demand was lost over the raised voices. On the screen, she could make out bodies moving to and fro, trucks and police cars. Not their own, she noted with a brief release of the tension that had unconsciously built inside her.

"Where?" she demanded.

"New Orleans," Katya muttered over her shoulder. "It's bad. Most of the nest is lost, but they think some children have holed up in the walk-in refrigerator. They're trying to get into it now. It's been locked from the inside."

Her skin crawled, the outpouring of fear and concern like a million spiders climbing up and down her body.

"Everyone is dead?" She turned and saw the fury on Katya's face. The way her eyes narrowed to pinpricks and the subtle buzz that exuded from her aura.

"Yeah. Brutal. A vampire attacking a nest. I'd suggest they thought it's only happening everywhere else, and they had adequate defences. Poor decision." Her answer might have been succinct, but it came out distinctly like a snarl.

Impotence wasn't an emotion Genny dealt with well. She clenched her fists and took a last glance at the screen, the need for the coffee she'd been about to make no longer foremost in her mind. "Has anyone contacted the local nests?"

Katya shrugged. "You know what they're like. Prickly and don't really welcome outsiders."

Turning on her heel, Genny hurried to her desk, gathered up her authorised weapons and keys. Almost to the door, she stopped when a voice called her name. She turned to see the boss frowning at her. "Be careful. They're on alert and won't be happy to see an outsider."

Perhaps not, she thought after nodding her thanks, but she was a Liaison officer. It was her job and calling. Immaterial of if they agreed, she'd do her best to ensure their safety.

At the car, she slid in and revved the engine. "Best to do this alone," she muttered and reversed out of her parking space. The roads were jammed, as they were pretty much all the time, so with a frustrated growl, she hit the lights and sirens.

Cars jockeyed to clear the way, but it took time, and her nerves shredded as she left the jam-packed areas behind.

Her phone beeped, her partner's name appearing on screen. "Where are you?"

"Heading for the House of al bin Habbad. I want to be sure they're—"

"You're mad," he interrupted. "You upset the *Yeux Secondes* already, and I doubt he'll be overly welcoming right now."

The reasonable tone only whipped the frenzy in her blood.

"Perhaps, but it's our job to ensure they're safe."

"Oh, come on, Genny. They're *vampires* and more than capable of keeping themselves safe."

His words battered her. Was that really how he felt? That they should stand alone? What would he do if he knew... Genny reined in her thoughts. *No need to go there*, she told herself.

She gripped the steering wheel tight. "Really? So what happened in New Orleans, then?"

Silence.

The turn loomed, and she indicated and drove up the long gravelled driveway. "Gotta go," she muttered and ended the call.

After she'd parked and run up the steps, she was stopped at the door. Two big and burly men waited, their frowns foreboding, but even more so their massive size.

"We're not accepting visitors right now," mumbled the larger.

She glanced up, noting the red of his irises. Vampires, both of them. Her inner cat nudged against the bonds she'd mentally wrapped around it.

Her hands flexed involuntarily, but she breathed out through her nose. "Officer Fernly, Liaison Division. I'm here to see either the *Yeux Secondes* or the master. Whoever will see me."

The larger man quirked an eyebrow. She reached for her shield, where it lay on her waistband. She raised it so he could see. He inspected it thoroughly and cast a glance to the man standing beside him.

The smaller vampire shrugged, stepped away, and she was sure he was talking mentally from the way both his eyes tracked to the left. Subtle tells, but she was used to them having spent years in a nest.

"Kharisma says let her enter."

The doors slid open, and she stepped inside. The foyer where she'd been earlier in the day was transformed. She guessed it was to prepare for whatever lay ahead. Tables and chairs dotted the enormous area, and vampires, more than she'd spied earlier, congregated around. She'd bet they were also armed.

The creature inside her stretched again, and the fear and concern took on the sense of a million spiders climbing up and down her body. Genny gritted her teeth together. Hard.

A woman broke away, stepped forwards, and extended her hand in welcome. "Kharisma," she greeted Genny. "You're to be escorted to David. Follow me, please."

Few words, but they clearly summed up the current state of the house. Readiness was key.

Genny followed, footsteps echoing, and they entered a small meeting room beside the *Yeux Secondes* office where she'd been just this morning. The table was round, and Kharisma settled herself beside David Jardin.

He glanced up as she entered the room.

Suddenly, Genny was overcome with nerves. How would they respond to what she'd come to say?

Silence gathered around her, lengthening and increasing her unease.

"Officer Fernly, how can we assist?" David grinned in a cold and forbidding fashion.

"I... uh, Kharisma and Mr Jardin, I'm here on behalf of the Liaison Division. We wish to offer our condolences and support in this time." She shifted on her feet, moving unconsciously as nerves crashed around her.

"We thank you, Officer." Kharisma inclined her head. The formality cloyed, and for a moment, Genny was sure she would pass out. Then she smiled. "Come, take a seat, Officer."

She joined them at the table. "The Liaison Division is very aware that the situation right now is grave and worsening. I hate to be difficult..."

Kharisma nodded. "I understand. There isn't much I can share, which I know you're aware of. You grew up in a house, I understand, so you know even I must abide by certain restrictions."

Shock stole her breath. "I... I didn't know you had made enquiries."

She smiled, but it wasn't condescending. It was friendly, and the cat in Genny inched a little closer to the surface.

"I didn't. Counsellor Cressida knew. She informed all of us." Kharisma extended her hands to indicate those gathered around the table.

"I see. Then you know..."

"A little. Only what I need to be aware of."

It was a sucker punch. Did that mean the master knew what she was? Did the *Yeux Secondes,* David Jardin? It was like someone poured a ghastly drink down her throat, coating it with a sour aftertaste.

"Fine," she returned. "But to be honest, with all the attacks and the escalation, how do we know who's behind this? How can we deal with them, and what do we tell the regular officers who may come face to face with these vampires?" *Heaven knows, the situation is pretty dire.*

Kharisma winced. "I understand your concerns. I will give you as much information as I can, and we've been asked by the Council to offer you any help. David here will be available to you. We need to clamp down on what's happening, but there appear to be two issues. The first, we are dealing with. It must be a vampire-led attack on the one we know as Attar. More details will be available soon. I can't share more." The woman smiled, and though it was apologetic, there was no way she didn't also understand it was a firm line.

"So, what else?"

"Attar is making vampires. Lots of them, but some are straying. They are hungry. The situation in New Orleans is not connected to them, and neither are the larger attacks. The one you helped, that was a stray."

Genny rubbed the ache forming between her brows. "Stray? I've never heard that term before."

"No. It's not used often. But we aren't talking about true rogues. These are turned and hungering. They don't belong in a nest, so they have no one to guide them, whichever way they choose to feed and live. To be candid, I'm not sure we have the manpower to deal with them and the situation with Attar. Everyone is hunting and searching. Everyone works together, but the strays are slipping through the cracks. If we could rely on the police via the Liaison Division, we have a hope of saving more innocents."

Kharisma's words fed the growing unease in her gut. "You want us to mop up what you can't cope with."

"I probably wouldn't have put it so bluntly." Kharisma swivelled. "I must leave. David will discuss in more detail with you what we know." Then the woman rose and left the room.

"I didn't expect you back here so soon, Officer Fernly." David's eyes gleamed in the artificial light.

"I didn't expect to receive any further assistance," Genny answered honestly.

He frowned. "Things are fraught. We lost an entire nest, and there's upheaval in other nests. Ours is growing far more rapidly than we could have expected, and with the change of *Yeux Secondes*, well, we're all a little... edgy."

Genny blinked at the candour of his words. "Indeed. So, tell me about this Attar. Who is he, and what is the situation?"

David grimaced. "We don't have a lot of information. He's an old vampire. We don't know quite how old, but he's dangerous. He's been able to hibernate for centuries from what we've gleaned. There's some suggestion he's one of the first vampires, which makes him truly dangerous. We have people researching and hunting, but he's sly and good at getting what he needs. His people are creating chaos, and no one is safe, not even in the nests."

"Why is he making vampires? Or at least more than anyone else?"

David shook his head. "My take is he's after power. Probably thinks he's more important than the greater sum of those alive. Isn't that the way with criminals?"

Genny bit her lip. "Sometimes, but this isn't a single lone gunman. This is a vampire, making more vampires, and they're killing. The injury and death rates are climbing, Mr Jardin. People are restive. They want vampires controlled." She wasn't game to say any kind of paranormal was lumped into the batch, because that opened doors no one wanted to investigate.

"How did you come to be in the Liaison Division?"

His question surprised her, and Genny blinked. "What?"

"How did you end up working with a division who are dedicated to liaising between all the varied species?"

"I... I came from a family of shifters." Really, it was a pride, but she didn't disclose what she was, because most of them refused to acknowledge her. Deep within, the cat hissed and demanded release.

"I gathered that much." She didn't ask, but he nodded. "It's there in your eyes. When you're agitated, they sort of contract into small slits." Now he smiled, and it was warmer. "It's very attractive."

She started. "What?"

His laugh was rich. Full bodied, like a well-aged merlot.

Inside her, the cat wanted to purr.

She clenched the muscles of her stomach, ensuring any physical reaction was contained and hidden.

"You don't like being reminded of your inner animal, do you?" The words were silky, almost seductive, and Genny didn't quite know how to answer. That was odd, because usually she'd be the first to remonstrate if someone enquired about her inner animal. It wasn't something a person did. The animal was private and their individual connection soul-deep.

"Look, I want to work with you, Officer. We got off on the wrong footing. Let me get you a coffee or tea, and we can talk."

She must have looked like a gasping fish, because surely her mouth was hanging open with surprise.

"I'm here on business. Stopping for coffee isn't really in my plan." She rose, wanting to get far away from whatever it was about him that left her so muddled and unable to think.

"Wait!"

His call stopped her retreat at the door. When she turned back, his face was filled with an earnest concern. "I didn't mean to offend you. I just would like to talk. We're not the most formal of houses, something I'm trying to get my head around. Please? Stay and I'll try to answer as many of your questions as I can."

Genny shook her head. "I'm needed back at the station." The words were lies, of course. She had to hide the fact that any sensible question had fled under the pressure of his smile and offer.

Back in the car, she gripped the wheel. "What the devil are you doing?" But even sitting there, staring at the house, she knew whatever it was driving her to make poor decisions couldn't be allowed to bloom. Because if it did, she was in for a world of pain.

CHAPTER 3

What the hell had he said to make her run? David had seen the hint of terror, and then she'd been up and off, out of her seat.

He sighed and turned his attention back to his work.

The hours passed quickly after her flight, and soon the night was dark. *Perhaps I should turn in, start fresh in the morning?*

Previously, before walking away from the nest his father had ruled with an iron fist, each day would have passed in the large commercial building, bustling with staff who knew their aspects of the business and ran it like a well-oiled machine. He'd have been taking briefings and making investment decisions in an office that reeked of money and class. His suit would have been an immaculate one-of-a-kind costing thousands of dollars, and he'd have had carafes of coffee on hand, while his personal assistant would have screened calls.

It was the position he'd been groomed for his entire life. His future secure and accepted while he attended the right schools, had the right training. Took the right wife.

"God!" He groaned, well aware that the time to examine decisions had long since come and been ignored.

Instead, David had run away from the memories and regrets, and the recriminations he should have faced. The ones no one had heaped upon him. He'd been a fool, blindly accepting his parents' machinations in his life.

Since he'd left there, he'd felt rudderless. Ill at ease.

He was needed here. With Daniel joining Cressida, they'd needed a stable guiding hand, but he wasn't the fit he'd hoped to be.

David knew he wasn't like the rest of the nestlings. Though he knew the business aspects inside out, and understood the intricacies of what was due to whom, he didn't fit in, as this nest was far more casual than he was comfortable with. First names were used by even the lowliest to address him. That had been a culture shock in the earliest days of joining the nest.

It wasn't what he was used to.

Oh, he did his job well enough. The nest was growing, the investments sound. He'd found several ways to increase the output of their manufacturing arm.

His heart just wasn't in it.

His mind returned to the woman who'd left in such a hurry.

Liaison Division. Javed had offered very little information, as had Kharisma. He wanted to know more about her—hell, it was more than that. Her memory gnawed at him. What was it about her?

"Papers won't wait," he muttered and glanced down, but they swam in front of his tired eyes.

He pushed back from the seat and moved from the meeting set-up, as exhaustion reminded him it was time to rest his body.

David made his way up the stairs, listening to the clank of feet on metal and wood. The human quarters were at the top of the building, while below were the reinforced bunker apartments of the vampires.

Tonight, Celina and Javed were with Cressida and Daniel, Xavier, and his sister, Hope.

His brain told him to change once he closed the doors to his private rooms, but waves of sleepiness washed over him, so he gave in and lay down. Sleep claimed him quickly.

Dusk had well and truly passed, and while she'd taken the time to rest earlier in the day, it had been neither relaxing nor refreshing. Genevieve felt the sap of energy in her bones as she wearily parked the vehicle once more behind the old cinder block building that housed the Liaison Division. Thankfully, they were set apart.

Cracking open the door was met with an equally jaw-cracking yawn. She staggered up the steps, only to stop short when the emptiness of the building caught her attention.

"What?" she demanded of Katya, who waited, jittery.

"There're children missing from the al bin Habbad house. No one knows where they've gone, but there're major concerns for their welfare and safety."

Energy revved inside her. "I should go—" she started, but before she could finish, Katya's eyes rolled, as they did when she was foretelling. "No. You'd be unwelcome." Then she squinted at Genny as the moment passed. "Trust me. That's a firm no."

Genevieve opened her mouth but stopped. Whatever Katya was, she was always insightful and was more often than not right with fraught situations.

"But perhaps I can..." She rose just as the boss entered the room.

"Sit down, Genevieve. Katya is right. This is not the time to run blindly into an unknown situation. We cannot interfere unless our help is requested. Particularly not at this point when there are human children involved." He spoke with such authority that she couldn't argue. The boss made the rules and enforced them. She had to abide.

She sank back down into the chair, but it didn't make the situation any easier to bear.

"I could help," she muttered.

Lottie, a witch who sometimes assisted in the department, bopped into the small room. "They'll find the girls soon." Then she grinned, and Genny shook her head. She'd definitely never been wrong before.

David woke to the sounds of searching. He rubbed aching eyes and staggered to his feet. Opening the door, he watched the barely controlled rushing of nestlings. He grabbed a woman by the arm and turned her to face him. "What's going on?"

"The three children? They're gone. They were with Kharisma earlier in the gardens. She left them to attend a meeting, but when she returned, they'd disappeared. She scented an unknown vampire, so they've called in Cressida, Daniel, Hope, and Xavier to follow the scent trail. In the meantime, Kharisma pointed out that there could be someone else here. We need to check carefully to make sure we're safe." The woman nodded and retreated.

His head ached, but no matter his own personal discomforts, he should be downstairs, if not assisting with the search, then at least marshalling sustenance for those who were on their return.

He pulled the door closed and headed down to the kitchen. Scents filled his nostrils, though not of food but burning. David hurried into the kitchen and noted pots on the stove, flames leaping and smoke filling the air. He sprang over, looking at the knobs. He'd spent little to no time in kitchens since his childhood but knew turning them either increased the flame or doused them. One by one he turned them off.

As he turned, a wild commotion and cries went up. "They've been found!" He didn't know who called out, but there were claps and cries of happiness. It filled him with hope. Perhaps all was not lost yet?

Stepping from the kitchen, he spied the cook and beckoned him over. "The pots on the stove were catching. I've turned them off."

"Damn. Thank you. I'll get someone to scrubbing the pots and arrange for food for those who require it," the cook answered.

"We'll need food for the searchers too." Though he'd already seen the goblets standing on the side, his experience was that they were always ravenous after a hunt. "They'll require filling with blood, and add a warmed carafe in case they wish more." He nodded to where they sat on a silver tray.

"Of course, David," the cook answered.

Satisfied, he moved to his office. He'd want to contact their security firm and find out how the incursion had been missed. It burned him that children, and especially those who were under the care of the nest he led, should be endangered.

The vampires stalked in, eyes shining with the scarlet gold of intense hunger and emotions.

Cook scurried forwards and Daniel stepped into his office while peace surrounded him. Once the door closed, he sighed and slumped against the wall.

Am I the best person to be leading them all? The question gnawed at him. He couldn't decide now, his own anxiety spiking, and he knew that would cause him to make poor decisions.

With that awareness in mind, he stalked to his chair and sank down into it, taking a moment. Then he spun the seat, reached for the lower of the small filing cabinets, and dragged out the file marked Security.

GENNY PICKED UP THE PHONE. "GENEVIEVE FERNLY."

"Officer Fernly. I'm ringing to ask if you'd be available to meet later today." Her informant's voice sounded shaky.

"Sure, Lolly. How about in an hour outside the Stop and Go?" The small coffee shop was more of a hole in the wall, but it was also anonymous and perfect for meeting a snitch.

"Yeah," the woman muttered, and the line disconnected. She'd been working with her for over a year, getting her to feel comfortable feeding information back, but Genny hadn't heard from her for a month or two before this.

"Just hope it's worthwhile." She opened the drawer where she kept her wallet. The snitch rarely wanted much, and the unwritten rule she used was no cash until the information was verified. It had taken her a while to find enough people who agreed to these rules, but the boss had been adamant, and it worked perfectly. They rarely wasted time with information that wasn't usable.

The Stop and Go was all the way across town, and she'd need to move now if there was any hope of making the meet. Traffic at this hour of the day could be a manic, she thought as she moved out, having scribbled a quick and somewhat cryptic note for her partner. She'd need to talk to the boss about that too. Her older, human partner was due to retire in several weeks and spent more time now clearing up paperwork than with her, and that suited Genny just fine.

The autonomy of working alone suited her.

The car groaned as she crept through the traffic, her eyes alert to anything suspicious, but when she reached the parking area, it was empty. Genny frowned. *Odd.*

Her hand automatically moved to her belt, checking to ensure her weapons were within easy reach as concern crept over her and she climbed from the car.

She caught sight of the woman she'd come to meet loitering beneath the sign hanging just beside the doorway.

Genny moved in, and Lolly followed her inside. They ordered their drinks and moved into a private seated area where she waited in silence.

"Vamps. Filthy lucre-toting bastards. They're everywhere at the moment, but there's a nest of six or seven. I've seen them hanging around the old mercantile building, but they're not following the normal rules. I seen them feeding and killing. They shouldna been here, ya know?"

Genny frowned. "The mercantile building? The empty one on the eastern side?"

"Yeah. Seen them coming and going. They also got a few humans now, keeping an eye out. Reckon they're Rocketmen."

The Rocketmen were an offshoot of one of the most dangerous human gangs in the region. If they'd somehow made an agreement with them, then things were really bad. Genny knew she needed to get the intelligence back to the boss and quickly.

Once the drinks arrived, she slipped a couple dollars into Lolly's hand. "Stay safe, and I'll be in touch soon. Keep your head down."

Lolly's gaze met hers. "I've done bad things in the past, but this is past what I'd do. I'm getting outta here, Fernly, and I don't want no cash, 'cause I've got friends with bigger friends, and they'll find me somewhere I can hunker down. You've done good. You're square with me. I appreciate that."

The woman waddled away as Genny watched.

The mercantile had been empty for years. It had once been a

thriving business for humans needing just about anything until a downturn had forced the family who owned it to walk away.

Now the building was in a state of disrepair, and its integrity was failing. Could she chance a drive by, or would that raise more questions? With a shake of her head, Genny decided that now wasn't the time. She'd need others to join her. Maybe even soft clothes and an unmarked car so they didn't raise questions. That and she knew Lolly bunked down somewhere around there. She'd give the woman time to clear out. It was the least she could do after being offered a freebie.

Once she'd reached the precinct, she took the steps two at a time and hurried inside.

"Hey, they found the kids" came from a corner, and she gave a sign of victory before knocking on the boss's door.

"Hey, got a minute?"

He was hunched over his desk and nodded. "Whatcha got?"

"My informant today told me she's found a group of vamps. They've hungry habits, but not nested. They're hooked in with a Rocketmen gang guarding them, living in the old mercantile building. It's condemned, and no one goes there, so it makes sense that they'd hole up there. I need to follow up but don't want to go alone."

"What about your partner?" He sat up, steepled his fingers, and stared at her.

Frustration rose, but she beat it back. Realistically, she knew this was about him making sure she knew what she was asking for and had drawn appropriate conclusions as to safety. "He's ready to retire, and working alone works best for me."

"We don't work alone, Genevieve," he answered.

The need to roll her eyes was difficult to banish, but she did. They'd been over her situation on more than one occasion. "I'm in a better position than when I joined the crew. I've come to terms with—"

"My crew. My terms. No one works alone. I know your partner is retiring, and I've been busy recruiting, and I think I've found you the perfect partner. He's a shifter too. You might even know him."

Her gut churned. *No. Oh no!* Her lips felt like concrete. "Who?" she asked.

"Julien Delacorte."

Oh God! Oh God! Oh God! How am I supposed to cope with this?

David stared at the meal before him. Somewhere in the long day, he'd considered eating, but now that the time had come, he couldn't raise any enthusiasm. The bowl of pasta congealed before him, and all he could do was stare at it.

Something made the hairs prickle at the back of his neck, and he looked up. *Who's watching?* Turning, he noted her in the doorway, her piercing green-gold eyes searching the room.

Tension flowed from her in waves.

He frowned and almost rose when she spied him. She firmed her mouth and started through the gathered throngs of nestlings.

"Mr Jardin." It certainly wasn't a query.

"Officer."

She took the seat opposite him and sat. "Hmm, that looks like you've waited too long." She pointed to the bowl, and he grimaced.

"Not overly hungry, to be honest."

"Ahhh."

David frowned. "Was there something specific you wanted to talk to me about?"

"Yes. Yes there is. I'm wondering if you've got a few people here, guards or the like, who'd be interested in joining me on a—" The air around her flashed. "—jaunt."

"A jaunt?" The word was an odd choice. "Where and why?" He leaned back in his seat and waited for her answer.

"Look, I got a call today. Someone in a position to see where some strays may hole up. I need to swing by. The problem is, I think they're being supported by a gang. My boss wants to me take someone with no experience in this area, but I need people with not just power but knowledge. The kind he"—she fiddled in her seat—"doesn't have."

He. Yet another tell. She had a few, from the fiddling and the flashing of eyes. Something about the "he" unsettled her almost as much as it did him.

"Who?" The word slipped out.

The woman opposite blinked. "I'm sorry?"

"Who's the 'he'?"

"Oh. An officer I knew long ago. Doesn't matter." She made to rise, and he reached out, covered her hand.

"Stay. Tell me more."

The flush of red tinged her cheeks, and her eyes glinted. "I shouldn't have come."

"Please."

She settled back in her chair. "Mr Jardin—"

"David," he corrected gently, and her mouth fell open. "Look, I know I'm thought to be strait-laced and pretty uptight. I'm trying. Work with me, okay?"

"Sure," she mumbled.

"So, you need help."

"I'm not sure that's quite how I put it. More like if you had people, humans, who've got training and skills and can be spared."

"I'll talk to Kharisma and ask around. When are we doing this?"

She started, and the chair scraped on the floor. "There's no 'we,' Mr Jardin."

"David," he corrected once again. "You use my people, you get me too. I'm not unable to defend myself, you know."

Now her eyes roamed over him, and the heat inside him rocked up to simmering. "I'm not sure you understand the depth of the dangers, David." He watched as she visibly settled herself, inhaling deeply and tightening, then loosening her fist. "These are the Rocketmen gang members. They're sly and won't hit you immediately. They'll wait until your back is turned, then attack your family."

David shook his head. Perhaps she was right, and they would launch a surprise attack, but on who? His parents? He didn't know where they were and certainly hadn't had any contact since the truth about his soon-to-be ex-wife had emerged. Hope? She was a vampire and had a legion of supporters and guards. Who did that leave? No one.

"Trust me," he said, "I've got no one who'd be unprotected."

She frowned. "No one?" He read the scepticism on her face. "Your parents?"

Whatever expression he responded with must have surprised her, as she reared back. "Did I cross some boundary there?"

"No. I don't have contact with my parents right now, and my sister and I... we've some fence mending to do. All my fault."

The surprise in her gaze melted away to something like understanding. "Ahhh, I see. I heard a bit about your ex-wife, but I didn't realise..."

For the first time, he wanted to explain. To offload some of the burden he carried. Would that scare her off?

That startling thought confused him further. "I'm not sure I want to talk about that."

"Sure. Look, do you want me to leave? I can—"

"No," David cut her off. "Let's grab a coffee and go outside. It's quieter there."

She followed him to the large coffee machine, poured herself a large mug, and followed him to the door. Outside, he blinked and led her to the side gardens. "We're working on a sensory garden for the children of the nest."

"Do you have kids here?"

"No, but Celina and Javed have the three they share their apartment with and I suppose will probably adopt in time, formally. But we've got a plan for the nest, including buying the houses around and making them part of the greater nest compound. Building multifamily units with a crèche on-site. Makes sense, as we'd like to move the office onto the grounds eventually, with only the manufacturing arm in town."

"Wow. You've been busy."

David blinked. "I suppose so."

He found a bench, and they sat down. "You don't sound like your heart is in it, though."

Maybe it was because she was an officer of the police, or perhaps she just had a kind of perception. He shook his head. "I really don't know what I want to do with my life. Before this, I let my parents decide, gave them the power to set the direction, and it didn't work so well."

She sighed. "I sort of know what you mean. I love my maman, but she'd have me married by now and making babies if I let her. But I don't want that." When he looked at her, she shrugged. "That's not totally it. I mean, there are other reasons, but I need to live my own life. Decide who I am before I make the kinds of long-term decisions she'd like me to make."

"And you like what you do?" It was written on her face, in the way she held herself and the determination to do what was right.

"I feel like I was born for the role. Protect. Serve. There's no higher calling, is there?" Genevieve—*Officer Fernly*, he reminded himself—informed him. Then she rubbed her chest.

"When were you injured?" The words escaped unbidden, and her face blanked.

"Pardon?"

"Now and then, you rub your chest, as if it hurts."

Her hands clenched, and a single long claw emerged. Not for the first time, he wondered if she realised just how much she was sharing when her emotions got the better of her.

"It was... something like that."

He didn't miss the way she corrected herself. But it intrigued him. Made him want to know more. Clearly she had issues.

Hell, so do you, idiot.

"I'm sorry," he murmured. "I didn't mean to put you on the spot like that."

CHAPTER 4

Genny sighed. Something about this man made her want to talk and confide. To see how he'd cope with her and what she really was. It wasn't wise, but the animal inside her urged her on.

"I'm a hybrid." The words tumbled from her mouth before she could call them back.

"And?" One simple word, but it encapsulated the entire issue. He didn't understand. Hell, he lived in a world of vampires, where humans were kept safe and the ugliness hidden behind a façade. Nothing like her reality. "Maman took several lovers. My brother, Bastien, is the son of her mate. I'm not."

He stared at her, expression blank.

"Cats can have more than one fuck in a heat session, right?" The coarse words flowed from her mouth. She needed to tell him all. It was brutal, but it was also her reality. "My maman was in heat. It was before she agreed to formally mate with my twin brother Bastien's father."

She stood, more than a little aware that her every movement betrayed the agitation she held inside herself. It had built and built over the years, and now she had to release it because there was no other option. It lashed at her. Saying the words and acknowledging them was necessary; otherwise, it felt like she'd explode.

"She was a party girl. One night, when the heat grew, she was out drinking with friends. She met a guy who she thinks was Irish, but she was drunk and never really told me much about him. She always said she couldn't discuss it." Genny swiped a shaking hand across her forehead. Now that she'd opened up, it just rushed at her like a dam where the wall had failed. "She took off with him for the night, then met Bastien's father the next day. Only she didn't know she'd already been impregnated. Nine months later, we were born. Dad—that's what I called him for fourteen years—thought we were both his until puberty. Then the truth came out. Maman had to leave the pride. She ran because he said she'd duped him, and he was viciously angry. I was no child of his, he said, and unworthy of his support and protection, making me a bastard with no standing in the clan. We hid until I turned eighteen, and on my birthday, she went back to him without me. Bastien went with her. I joined the academy, and that's my story."

It wasn't, though. Not in its entirety, because the story of her, and Julien was something else. The thing she would never get over because she was scarred. Not just emotionally but also physically.

"She wants me to come home. Bastien is taking a mate, and I may return for the ceremonies that come before and the Joining. I don't know if I can." Her breath caught, and in that moment, truth and reality aligned as never before. "Papa—my grandfather—passed two years ago, and the edict has been retracted. I could go back, but I don't know that I want to."

She turned, and he was there, standing behind her. His face shadowed, yet all she felt radiating from him was understanding and acceptance.

"Why, Genevieve?" He spoke gently, as if not to spook her, reaching out his hand to her.

"Because they broke me. It took so long to pull together what I have. What I am now." Damn that hitch in her voice and the way she shook. Terror careered deep within her at the depth of emotions welling inside. Shaking her head, she pulled back, away from David and the heat that warmed the icy centre of her being.

He didn't release her, instead followed where she led.

No one had ever wanted her once they knew what she was. And wasn't.

"I could come with you." Five small words, but they wound around her like an embrace, filling the empty chasm inside her.

She wanted it. Needed it with an urgency that surprised and overwhelmed.

"Don't...," she whispered, but he gathered her closer, and their lips brushed together by chance. Electricity arced between them, and the cat inside roared its pleasure at the touch and demanded more.

"Genevieve," he murmured, settling his mouth on hers more firmly as he fitted his frame to hers. It felt... good.

She tugged away, refusing to acknowledge the need that raised its head, because if she allowed it to grow, she might never recover when he left.

"Don't. Please, Mr Jardin." The words snapped him still, just as she'd calculated in the split second before saying them.

He let go. "Forgive me." His face was once more as impassive as the usual mask he wore, but in the depths of his gaze, she spied hurt and something more. Rejection.

Before she could do anything else, he spun on his heel and left her there alone in the courtyard.

Burning eyes settled on a form at the end of the garden. A child.

The hairs at her nape rose.

What the child was, she didn't know, but she had to get out of there now.

CHAPTER 5

David worked like a demon, hoping to banish thoughts of a womanly body and soft lips.

Night came, and with it the awareness of someone in the doorway, watching him.

He raised his head and started with surprise. “Hope.” Uncertainty about how to welcome her raced through him. Years of lies and anger simmered between them still.

“Do you mind?” Her face softened as she stepped into the room. “You’ve settled in, then?”

Stilted conversation, but he deserved no more. “Uh, yes, thanks.”

“I came to talk to you. See if you’re okay. Cressida made a comment last night, but I wanted to check on you.”

“Ah, she made a similar comment to me, I’d guess. Last of the line and so on.”

Hope nodded. “Yes.”

“I’m fine.”

He fisted his hands. Fury at their parents and Alexa, because they’d been close once, he and Hope. Now it was like a damn wall lay between them, and neither seemed to know how to get past it.

Hope gave a tiny nod and retreated, and for a moment, he felt the urgency to follow her. He stopped himself, pouring every ounce of will into the admonition. She didn't need him.

David picked up the card that lay by the phone.

Dialled the number.

"Yes?" a sleepy voice filled the air.

"When did you plan to check the mercantile building? I'll have men ready."

"What?" The word was more alert, as if she'd just realised who called and what was being said.

"When, Genevieve?"

Silence filled the air as he waited, aware she hadn't hung up. Rustling echoed. "Uh, not tomorrow. Tuesday, say ten in the morning. We could meet at the precinct."

"Fine. Cars?"

"Bring your own," she muttered.

"See you then." He hung up, stared at the phone. Then he smiled.

GENNY CURSED INTO THE DARKNESS. "WHAT THE HELL WAS THAT all about?" Rubbing at the now aching spot between her eyes didn't relieve the pressure.

A glance at the clock assured her it wasn't worth going back to sleep. With another, even more vicious curse, she climbed from the bed. Letters that had been waiting for her when she'd returned from the precinct that morning caught her attention.

One, the address in elaborate script, captured her eye. "Oh, Maman!"

Tears pricked her eyes, well aware of what lay within the heavy cream parchments. She scooped it up on the way to the fridge and tugged out yet another steak. Blood filled the bag, and she sighed, popping the envelope onto the bench before tossing the meat into the pan on the stove. She covered it with pre-made stock and added a few frozen veg, then set it on a very low heat. Searing the outside seemed to satisfy her almost human half, while the animal within relished the bloody centre. "If only the rest of my life was so balanced," she muttered.

At the sink, she rinsed, then dried her hands and picked up the envelope once more.

"Funny, the weight of it." Sliding a nail under the flap, Genny broke the seal.

She slid the heavy card from the envelope, then peered back in. Something wrapped in paper remained. With care, Genny slid it from the base and peeled back the wrapping, revealing a handwritten note.

Ma petite bebe,

I should have given this to you long ago. However, with Bastien now looking to the future, I must face the sins of the past. I must explain my past, though it will not be easy.

Your father—for there was only ever one other than Luca—gave me this the night we came together. Said it would one day meet a need.

It never occurred to me that the need may not be my own, but yours.

Bastien and I both want you to return, even if only for the ceremony, but at the end of the day, this decision is yours. However, we must talk, and this is best done face to face, daughter.

Call me.

Your loving mother,

V

She glanced at what she'd uncovered. A very large gold coin, which winked in the light. She sighed. "A coin? What's this supposed to mean?"

True, it caught her eye, the way it winked and shone as if a new penny. Her fingers wanted to curl around it.

Her knee banged against the cupboard. "Shit!" She growled and realised she'd stepped forwards without thinking. "That's odd."

Genny tossed down the invitation, and it covered the coin. The sudden need to hold and caress it melted away, and she breathed deeply as the stink of burning meat filled her nostrils.

"Oh, no!" She tugged the pan from the stove, switching the knob to Off. "Gods damn it!" The growl married with the lurch of her belly and the knowledge that she'd somehow allowed herself to become bewitched more than irked.

Tossing the meat and veg into the trash, she retreated from the kitchen. "Shower. Change. Get out of here."

She hurried through the necessaries, but the pull to the coin remained, like a bloody tether between it and her.

It was only in the car, distance between them, that she drew a breath. The car paired with the cell, and she stabbed her finger at the autodial.

"Bebe?" Her mother's voice floated along the wind.

"What the hell is that coin, Maman?"

She sighed. "I don't know, Genevieve, but I had this feeling you needed it. I meant to give it to you when you mated, but—"

"It entranced me, Maman. I burnt my steak and banged my knee." God, she sounded like a stressed and sulky teen.

"What? Why are you cooking?"

"Maman, we've been over this many times. I need more than meat and bone..."

"Because you're not fully—"

"Yes. I know what I'm not." The regret in her mother's voice almost broke Genny, so she bit out the last word more than she meant to. Shame washed over her. "I'm sorry for that. Look, I'm going to grab some food and head into the office. You're right though, we need to talk. About what I *don't* know."

"I... I understand, *bebe,*" her mother answered.

The sadness bit at Genny. "*Je t'aime Maman*," she said, then ended the call.

One moment, then another passed before Genny turned the key in the ignition and drove from the parking lot.

DAVID TRIED TO APPLY HIMSELF TO THE BEST INTERESTS OF THE NEST over the next few days. He met with the supervisors, met with the bank. He even met with the builders and architect working on new drawings to expand the house itself. With the purchase of the three neighbouring properties, everything was moving forwards at pace.

He just didn't feel so darned enthusiastic about his tasks, though.

Tuesday morning, he opened his wardrobe, tugged out a pair of well-worn jeans, a collared shirt, and a leather jacket from the very back, where he'd hidden them moving to the nest. These were clothes he'd owned long before Alexa had stuck her claws into him, the sort his mother deplored.

He teamed them with boots. Heavy soled and reinforced, if they got into trouble, at least a blow would hurt. And if he stepped in something...

Waiting on the bottom step, ten men and a tiny woman hovered.

"We should go." He motioned them forwards.

The large people mover proceeded, followed by another. Without the cresting of the house, they could almost pass for anonymous. *Almost*, except the gleam of chrome and the elegant lines screamed money. There wasn't much he could do about that.

The group split into two sets. With the keys in his hand, David climbed into the driver seat. By agreement, nestlings took the very rear seats, and with a rev of mighty engines, they moved out of the driveway and towards the road.

The weight of his car required David to concentrate and find the rhythm. "I think we should order another couple of these. The weight will make them resource hungry, but looking at the specs, I like their defensive value," he told the man sitting nearest him.

"I thought you might. We're tweaking the tires too. Found some that are combat suitable. Given the uncertain times and some alliances we're discovering, I think these will sell well."

He grunted. Another income stream would certainly assist the house.

Traffic was reasonable, and by the time the car swung into the parking area within the precinct, he realised they'd made up time. "I'm going in. Stay here and monitor the cars." It wasn't so much an order as a firm suggestion.

He took the stairs at a run, having once before visited the Liaison Division—straight after Alexa's arrest. She'd been brought to this building before she'd been officially tried at a joint sitting of the vampire Council and human judiciary.

Cells out the back were carefully reinforced to hold many species.

The only one they didn't hold were vampires, but given the robust nature of the vampiric trial system, agreements had been put in place, allowing vampires to deal with their own.

Alexa had straddled both sides with crimes against vampires and humans. In a historic decision, both sides had come together to hear the evidence and pass judgement on her. Now she was facing the term of her natural life in a maximum-security cell block somewhere overseas.

Once inside the door, he stopped. A man at the desk scowled. "Mr Jardin. Can I assist you?"

It took a moment for the name to come to mind. "Uh, no thank you, Lieutenant Belarmino. I'm here to meet with—"

"Officer Fernly. Yes, she and her team are coming now." His voice echoed, hoarse and growly, and not for the first time, David wondered exactly what the man was. Of course, he couldn't ask. That was beyond rude, and the dictates of his upbringing didn't allow for that.

David heard commotion and peered over the lieutenant's shoulders. There she was, face pale and drawn but very much focussed. Around her was a group of four other officers.

Her gaze settled on his, and he noted the way her face tightened. She stopped at the desk, indicated that the others precede her, and stared at him.

"Officer, I have two vehicles downstairs. If you'll join me."

"I said I'd prefer you didn't attend," she muttered, and he couldn't help a grin.

"You did, but I also told you, where they go, so do I."

"Huh," Belarmino growled. "If you've finished your foreplay or byplay or whatever, go. Some of us have other work to attend to."

David did not extinguish his smile but noted the narrowing of her eyes. He trailed her down the steps and watched as she circled the vehicle.

"I don't know this make." She bent down, inspected the wheel arches and windows, ran her fingers along the paintwork. "Where did you get this?"

"Both are prototypes. After the recent attacks on both nests and house vehicles, we began work on reinforced cars." He shrugged. "Every house will want one if we can make them right."

She stayed still for a moment, then nodded. "Makes sense. Who's driving?"

David smiled. "Me."

Genevieve climbed into the passenger seat. "Comfortable," she commented as he slid behind the wheel.

"We aim to please."

The car moved smoothly as he waited for Genny to instruct where they'd go, though traffic increased the longer they drove.

When they moved into an older section of town, he slowed at her request.

"Turn down this street," she murmured and lifted a small camera to her face.

"This what you need to see?" He indicated to an old dilapidated building where three burly men loitered. He noted the black leather vests they wore, but the air about them... it reeked of menace.

"Yessss." The word was little more than a hiss.

One man outside the building caught sight of the vehicles and nudged the others. They straightened up and moved towards the front awning.

Something about the way the men moved had Genny's heart thumping madly. "See the patches on their chest? Left-hand side?" She snapped another picture. "They're Rocketmen."

She knew them well, having had more than one run-in with them. The ugly sons of bitches were bad to the core, and the last time she'd dealt with them, she'd learned they had at least one shifter in their midst and likely more.

On her chest, the scar pulsed, a leftover of that dreadful night and hideous altercation. It reminded her of the danger they faced.

"We should move on," she said after realising David had pulled the car to a stop opposite the building.

"We're fine," he muttered.

"What? No, we need to move."

Two of the three men lumbered onto the street, the third raising a phone to his mouth.

"This is dangerous." Now her nerves frayed.

"Nah, it's all good."

Genny turned, dismay turning to horror when he smiled at her.

"Mr Jardin..."

A hand landed on her shoulder. "We're fine. These cars are pretty close to indestructible," the man behind her offered.

When she inspected the driver, she noted something. A kind of enjoyment as he watched the men on the road.

One tugged a snub-nosed pistol from his pocket.

Aimed.

Heart in her throat, Genny gulped.

The impact came with a dull thwack, a couple marks on the windscreen, but nothing else.

"What you can't see are the reinforcements of the glass. Carefully reinforced. It's the tweaks that aren't obvious that will pay off in the long run." David's voice was low, and she leaned forwards.

"What the hell are you talking about?"

He smiled and waved to the thug, the man's face growing darker. "The long-term aim is to sell these vehicles to houses and law enforcement. This one is about as bulletproof as you can get. The reinforcements are, shall we say, special."

The second thug came up beside the vehicle and tried to open the door. David peered at the man. "Pass me the camera," he said.

With nerveless fingers, she handed it to him and watched as David snapped the thug's portrait, then did the same with the first one, his face now in the shape of a snarl.

"Got enough, Officer?"

Her gaze was filled with the moves of the third as he ducked inside, then returned with something large and barrel-like.

"Uh, we should leave," she demanded. No matter how reinforced David might suggest the vehicle was, there was no way they'd survive what was coming.

He glanced in the direction she looked and smiled.

Smiled!

It was filled with relish and pleasure. Her gut curdled.

"We'll be fine."

"That's an A58Z Rocket Launcher. Capable of—"

"Yes, I know, Officer. We're still safe," the nestling from the back seat said.

No matter what he said though, it didn't make her feel any more secure or safe inside this box with the *Yeux Secondes* or his people.

They're mad! They must be. The safety of her people slammed into her mind. A quick glance back showed her the car behind remained in place, as if it too were waiting for whatever might come.

"Mr Jardin..." She needed to urge him to leave. Get out of there before it was too late. She turned back, facing the front, and stopped talking at the view before her.

The two thugs who'd been trying to get into the car backed away, their gazes feral. Gleeful. Terror seized her, worrying every nerve inside her body so it crackled and hummed.

A boom echoed, and the car rocked as something crashed into it.

Genny grabbed David's hand and squeezed, sure this was it. The absolute end. She closed her eyes tightly together and held her breath while the rapid drumming of her heart signalled a spike of adrenaline.

Seconds passed.

Long seconds that became fraught moments.

Her ears rang, and she opened her eyes.

"Like I said, safe. I know the capability of these vehicles, checked the specifications myself, and worked with Banks here to strengthen them. But let's head on now, shall we? You've seen enough?"

She nodded mutely, because what else was there to say? But as they drove off, she watched the men, knowing they'd probably opened a Pandora's box with this altercation.

The drive back was mostly silent as Genny evaluated everything she'd found out.

"Vampires holed up in the mercantile is a big problem. I can talk to the Council, but we'd need help from the Liaison Division and police to deal with the Rocketmen, since they aren't under our jurisdiction," David said.

She bit her lip and looked out the window. Again, he was right.

"I think I should talk to the boss. You best come in with me."

"I'll send the rest home, then. Just keep Hansen here, in case something comes up and we need to send the car home."

She blinked. What did he think was going to happen? That they were going to rout them immediately? "It shouldn't take long."

He grunted, and she waited out the rest of the trip in silence.

DAVID GLANCED AT THE NEAR SILENT WOMAN BESIDE HIM AND TRIED to work out what she was thinking. True, maybe he had shown off a little, but the car held up exactly as he'd expected it to.

Once they arrived at the precinct, he gave orders for all except Hansen to head back to the nest in the other vehicle. Hansen grinned. "I'm going to grab a bite to eat, then settle in. I've got a lecture to catch, so I'll do that in the back of the vehicle." Hansen had been his co-conspirator in the early days of designing the vehicle and had followed him from the nest he'd grown up in to the al bin Habbad nest. They weren't close, but they were partners. "Oh, and I've got a practical workshop tonight in town, so I won't be available."

David nodded. "We'll go attend to this, then grab lunch. I'll check in later."

David and Genny went up the stairs, and he placed his hand against her spine. An old-fashioned act, but it came naturally.

The woman before him stilled, muscles tight beneath the light touch. "Uh, Mr Jardin?"

He felt the echoes of her words in the vibration of her body, and his tightened in reaction.

"You can... step back."

Her head continued to face forwards, but for some wild reason, he got the feeling she wasn't really looking at the object of her gaze.

"Oh." He tugged his hand away and shoved it into his pocket, unwilling to consider why he still felt heated where he'd touched her.

Genevieve shoved open the door, and he ducked in behind her, trailing her to an office where she knocked precisely twice. The rapping echoed in the sudden silence.

"Come" came from within, and they entered the dark room. The hulking lieutenant hunched over a desk, his eyes gleaming in the dark. "You've found something?"

Settling into a chair, she tugged another beside it and showed David should sit, and he followed her direction, though the seat was hard and unyielding.

"Thanks to Mr Jardin, we ascertained that, yes indeed, the Rocketmen are guarding the mercantile. What we couldn't see is whether there are vampires in there. My informant, however, was quite clear. She'd seen them, and I trust her. We need to go back, possibly as early as this evening, and see if that's the case."

David sat up at that. She hadn't so much as mentioned going back at night. When the vampires were active. That was deadly thinking.

Before he could get a word out, the boss held up his hand. *"You will go back tonight. You will face danger. There is more and there is less than you hope to find."*

Immediately, David knew the lieutenant was allowing his precognition skills free rein.

"Sir? Is that the okay, then?"

The lieutenant nodded. "Yes, take Jardin and some men with you. We need evidence before we can address the council." His gaze narrowed. "When were you last off duty, Fernly?"

She blushed, a very becoming shade of pink. "I'm fine, sir."

The lieutenant grunted. "That's not what I asked. Take the afternoon as downtime after you brief your team. I want an update tonight. I'll authorize a team of five"—he grinned—"since Jardin will want to tag along." The man looked at David. "You still good with a sword and gun?"

David smiled. "I keep in practice, shall we say?"

Once more Fernly bristled, but he shrugged, telling himself he'd explain that and more to her over lunch.

They left the office, and Genevieve instructed him to "take a chair" and she'd be right back. Right back was forty-five minutes later.

However, he used the time to contact his office, giving instructions for the evening shutdown. He'd return later, he explained. "I will return with Hansen, but I can't be sure when. I've got one prototype and will use that for transport."

"Of course, sir. I also believe the master and Celina will be absent this evening."

David frowned.

"Have Kharisma ensure the nest is secured, then, and send the specs for the building to my phone. I want to check the security schematics again since they've been tweaked."

"Very well, David. I'll see you in the morning, then."

The line disconnected, and he frowned. That his second lived in a unit miles from the nest wasn't optimal, but it was the best he could do right now. Space was limited, and it was why most of the rooms were sparsely furnished. With fifty humans all employed in essential house-centric tasks, and forty-seven vampires in the basement, every inch of the building was pressed into service.

They might be fast-tracking the building of the smaller multifamily units around the main house, but the urgency that drove him still wasn't enough to ensure they'd be done as quickly as he might desire.

Fernly reappeared, and he stood. "We should find something to eat." She opened her mouth, but he shook his head, stopping her remonstrations. "I hear there's a nice little Italian place just around the corner."

Her eyes glittered. "I have other things I need to attend to," she growled.

"I'm sure you do, but tell me, you eat, right? We could find that Fusion place with nice juicy steaks if that's your preference."

Now she hissed. "Italian is fine, since I doubt I'm going to shake you off."

He would have reached for her, taken her hand, but she stalked to the door and wrenched it open. Instead, he settled on simply saying, "After you."

The acknowledgement that he was railroading her was damning, but more to the point, he felt the urge to get to know her more, and that drove his behaviours. He'd have to atone for that sin, he thought.

Outside, they moved to pass the car. "I just need to check on

Hansen," he said, and they stopped. He rapped on the door, and the window slid down. "Need anything?"

"Nah, got a drink and the tablet. These things go for hours," the younger man said. "Have a pleasant lunch." Then the window slid back up, but not before David saw the speculative gleam in the other man's gaze.

"Come on, let's go," Genevieve muttered, and David turned.

Faced with her back, the luscious curve of her backside, and the ruthless precision of her braid, he considered it a good day.

CHAPTER 6

Frustration coursed through Genny's body. She was in a small dark Italian restaurant, drinking soda water and waiting for the bowl of Bolognese to arrive. The salad long since gone. As she'd told her mother, she needed more than meat and bone in her diet.

"So, how did you come to join the Liaison Division?" David sat opposite her, and the dark stubble now colouring his jawline, the deep green of his eyes, and the subtle scent of maleness were picking apart the small vestiges of brainpower she had left.

"I joined the force, but most police have no clue about the depths of paranormal species. It was difficult because I'm more than human, and some questioned my strength and speed. Something I can't help, or hide."

Oh, she remembered the day it all came crashing down.

Julien, the man she'd thought would be her partner both in life and at work, had been eating a steak. Rare. Just the way he liked it. He'd frowned and sniffed the air. "You're really not like any other female I know," he muttered, his grey eyes gleaming.

"I'm not. Julien, I have to tell you the truth."

"You've not told me everything?" He waggled his brows, and she laughed nervously. His grin urged her confession.

"When we met your mother, you told her..." Oh God! *The words stuck in her throat, and she cleared it. She adjusted the camisole she wore, knowing how sexy he found it when she slipped the nearly transparent material on after sex. "I'm a cat shifter, yes, but Maman... she had two partners within the same heat cycle."*

"Sexy mama! When do I get to meet her?" His laugh soothed some of the raggedness that filled her.

"That's just it. She met someone. But he... he wasn't a shifter."

Julien's hand stilled, and his eyes narrowed. "What. Do. You. Mean?"

Her blood thickened and cooled. "I'm..." She gulped, twisting her hand in the soft material. "I'm not just a cat shifter, but I don't know what else, though. Maman said... She said he was a paranormal, but she didn't find out what."

A sudden chill invaded the room as Julien tossed the rest of the steak to the plate. "What the fuck?" He lurched away. "You're not pure. You led me on, Genevieve." Fury threaded his voice, and she wanted to shrink through the floor.

"No! No, I just didn't tell you—"

"You fucking lied *to me. Withheld knowledge. Why? So I'd mate with you? I planned to. Tonight I was going to ask you." Disgust surged in every word. "I've got to go." He reached for his pants and shirt, and Genny raced around the table.*

"Please, Julien. I wasn't hiding it. Maman counselled me—" She gripped his hand, and he flung her away.

"Don't touch me! Filthy creature!"

Shards of ice penetrated her chest as if he'd stabbed her. "Please, Julien."

"No. No more. I don't know you or want you. No shifter in his right mind would want a mutt."

Mutt. A filthy half-breed, and the ultimate insult to their kind.

"I was looking to leave the team I was part of. Needed a new challenge. I knew of the Liaison Division, and one day, I got the courage to wander in the front door. The boss was there, though he wasn't the senior officer. It was a woman before, and she was a real hard-nosed bitch, to be honest, but she was retiring. Boss had already been appointed, and there was an opening, so since the timing was right, and I had the skills they were looking for, I jumped."

He cocked his head to the side. "Just like that."

She blinked, because deep inside her was a yearning to tell him everything. Every bitter truth that had made her so distrustful. She wanted to trust him, and that made him doubly dangerous.

"Something like that," she muttered, ducking her head, but not before she noted the frown between his eyes. Whatever she'd said, it hadn't sat well. "What about your story?"

"Ah, well, I'm sure you've heard the story about my situation. The only son who grew up in the bosom of my family and was given every opportunity to succeed. Study and work were easy, and I was trained from birth to take control of the nest as a future *Yeux Secondes*. My wife was hand-picked and perfect. Beautiful and talented." His hands moved, and she watched them, aware they were long and tapering. "My sister, Hope, was an innocent who I allowed to be alienated, belittled, and dehumanised because I listened to the harpy I'd married while my father was in cahoots with Alexa. Even after she learned the truth, my mother didn't give a damn."

His voice turned ragged and bitter. Genny reached out, took his hand because no one deserved to live with regrets and hate for mistakes they couldn't own by themselves forever. She leaned closer and considered the self-loathing on display. Inside, the emotions she'd built a hard shell around peeked out. "Surely not?"

He shook his head. "By the time it was done, I had no family, no relationship, and my name was a tattered mess." He closed his eyes briefly, and she wondered if it was to stop him seeing derision or whatever emotion he expected from her.

"Mr Jardin—"

"David," he corrected.

"Fine!" His eyes opened, and she captured his gaze. "David, anyone who's aware of what happened knows you were fed lies by your wife and parents. It's what you do afterward that matters. I know you've moved on. You're assisting with the building of a new nest and trying hard to change. I can see that." She smiled, felt the curving of her lips.

His eyes widened and searched her face as heat arced between them, like an invisible connection. "Genevieve..." He shrugged as if lost for words.

"David, no one can get through life alone. Loneliness eats you up. Swallows you whole, and if you surrender to it..." She shrugged now.

"You've been there. Done that." It wasn't a query so much as a statement.

"I learned long ago that hybrids like me don't have a place in the natural order of shifters." Leaning back into the seat, Genny studied the man opposite and, for the flash of a second, wished it weren't a truth.

"That's not true." His gaze bored into her. "Not at all."

"I'm a *mutt*, David. Unworthy and unwelcome."

When he flinched at the vile word, she sighed. Once again, the truth of her birth would stop any chance of a relationship forming. Not that there could be one. He was above her pay grade.

"You're no mutt. You're beautiful and strong. A protector. Don't let anyone tell you anything else."

Now she laughed. "A mutual therapy session?"

He smiled, and his features lightened. "Whatever it takes, Genevieve. Tell me about this lilt in your voice."

She laughed. "Maman was born in France nearly two centuries ago. I guess a bit of that rubbed off on me."

"You weren't born here?"

"No. Down south, but when Maman was sent away, she went north. We lived there for about five... six years. Maman returned, and I settled somewhere in the middle because I needed to be me." *Away from the hate and threats.* She kept the thought to herself. He didn't need more right now, and she wasn't yet ready to face the fact that there was a driving need to tell him everything.

His gaze narrowed. "There's more though, isn't there?"

She blinked. "Pardon?"

"I've seen those called mutts before. They're threatened. Were you?" As if he could see within her soul, his brow creased with anger. That frightened her more, because what else could he see? Discern?

"You know, I'm sure our food should have been delivered here by now." Genny smiled, though it was false and bright. She knew he wasn't fooled by her attempts to deflect, but she didn't want to discuss it any further.

It was as if by magic when the food arrived.

They ate in silence, both watching the other but neither making the next move.

It made her jittery. Uncomfortable.

By the time they'd finished, she could cut the tension between them with a knife.

The bill came, and he quickly grabbed it, filled out the paper, and handed it back.

"I intend to pay for my lunch," she added.

"I wanted to eat here, so I believe it's my responsibility to pay."

"An ancient and not really PC stand, though."

He shrugged. "Perhaps, but it's the way I work."

That left her dumbfounded. It wasn't a date. But she wouldn't push right now. Another chance would arise where she could even the balance.

With that in mind, once the folder was returned, they stood and left the restaurant.

CHAPTER 7

David learned a lot about Genevieve Fernly during the afternoon. She didn't like to waste words. The woman was driven but compassionate and, like him, was all alone in the world in all the ways that mattered.

By three thirty, they'd returned to the office, and while he worked on his tablet, Genevieve worked like a demon, preparing a report, then the briefing. The team came together, and he raised a brow at the make-up. A lumbering man he was sure might be a bear shifter. Another was slight, but the glint in his eyes was dangerous. David couldn't hazard quite what he was, apart from deadly.

Genevieve, tiny but quick, and bringing up the last spot, a man she walked wide circles around. That caught his attention.

He watched the interaction, and clearly the last man was new and untried in the team.

When the man attempted to sit nearest Genevieve, David's hackles rose. "Excuse me, but that's my seat," he said smoothly.

The man stared at him. "Julien Avarre. You are?"

"*Yeux Secondes* of House al bin Habbad. David Jardin." He didn't extend his hand because the man appeared to think he had some connection to Genevieve, and that ignited a deep and strange protectiveness towards the woman he wanted to get closer to.

When Genevieve glanced at him, there was relief in her gaze, and he wondered at that. At least until everyone settled. Then she assumed a mantle of control.

Methodically, she walked them through what they knew, circulated the printed images she'd taken earlier, and shared the intelligence she'd received from her "snitch," as Genevieve called the unnamed person.

By the end, he felt he knew exactly what would happen. When the team stood, so did he. They headed in all directions, retrieving—he guessed—firepower and protective clothing. Genevieve excused herself only to return moments later with a large ballistic vest and helmet. "You come with me, you wear these."

The vest was bulky and rimmed with high visibility striping. He wanted to refuse, but the look on her face told him that without it, he'd be excluded. So he took the vest, muttered a "Thank you," and set about donning it while watching her do the same.

Her fingers fumbled on one clasp, and without thinking, he reached out and attended to it.

Their eyes caught, a zap of electricity arcing between them again. He noted the way her lips parted, the flash of awareness in her eyes.

David stilled.

The door opened, and in walked Julien Avarre.

"I was..." The man stopped and looked over the tableau.

David took a moment, swiped a curl that had come loose and draped over her cheek. Then he stepped back with a grin. "All done, Officer."

She blushed and grimaced. "Thanks." The breathless quality of her voice had Avarre frowning.

David guessed it was jealousy and couldn't help but feel buoyed by the thought.

They headed down the stairs, and the larger man looked at the vehicle. "I don't know this car make."

Suppressing a smile was difficult, David admitted to himself, when they looked it over and declared it was "pretty damned good."

"It's an early prototype. We intend to add further plating and shielding, and we're actively looking for ways to make it lighter," he explained.

The giant grunted and continued his inspections along with the other officers. Finally pleased with what they saw, the officers climbed inside, their packages balanced on legs and in the vehicle's rear.

He drove smoothly in the gathering gloom, stopping only to drop the first three officers at the location Genevieve had declared would be best.

"We'll have others standing by in preparation," she told them before the doors opened and the officers alighted. "They aren't necessarily aware of the full gamut of paras, so be careful. Our job is simply to capture and neutralize the vampires. The gang members will pose a significant threat, but the intelligence we've gathered leads us to believe they actually leave the vicinity once night falls. So, we need to find positions, hunker down out of sight until they leave, then move quickly."

Three would enter through the back, just in case anyone ran, and the rest through the front. Their backup would arrive soon, and David felt sure she wouldn't begin the action until everyone was in place.

He parked the car in the small laneway nearby. Watched as Genevieve positioned herself, eyeglasses raised, scanning the movements. He monitored the time, aware the day was ending and soon it would be time for the vampires to rise. Motorbikes roared, the sound of them splitting the silence. Seven bikes zoomed past, their passengers dressed in black and their masks painted with devils and bloodied Grim Reapers. None wore full face masks, but he guessed most humans would find them terrifying.

"Look alive, everyone. Vests on, and make sure UV guns are set to stun. If we can take them, that would be best. No chances taken. I want you all coming home tonight."

She suited up, and David struggled to pull on his own. Genevieve swiped his fingers away and expertly fastened the tabs before jamming the helmet on. "You may be a good fighter, but you don't take chances."

They climbed from the vehicle, and he watched her cast a glance to the building, then back, as if taking stock one last time. She inhaled.

Clicked the talk button on her comms device. "Let's go. Quietly to the doors. Three clicks for ready."

They moved, clutching guns at their sides, while his hand grasped the hilt of his sword. She hadn't allowed him a UV gun, and he wasn't sure if that pleased or irritated him more.

In position, flanking the doorways, they waited, anticipation coating the air.

Click. Click. Click.

"Go! Go! Go!" Genevieve called, and they moved quick as lightning, boots thudding on the old floors. David followed the rest, just as they'd agreed.

Growls and howls echoed, followed by a scream of fury.

Every muscle tensed, and suddenly a man stood before David, anger darkening his brow. He moved at a speed the eye couldn't follow, and instinctively, David raised his sword, more than aware of the copper tipping the edge, deadly to vampires.

The vampire lunged, and David caught him, a glancing blow but enough for the vampire to tug back and bare his fully extended canines.

The vampire advanced again, fury and pain clear in the pale, sweating visage. He charged, and David raised his sword, ready to parry. A nail, sharp as a razor, grazed David, and he hissed.

He spun, ready for another pass when a black cat struck. Eyes golden green and wide, its mouth open and ready for the now darting vampire.

Before David could thrust it aside, the vampire tackled the cat, and a crunch and then awful silence descended around him.

The cat shivered, gave a single snarl. A wicked ripping sound filled the air.

As he waited, the skin of the cat melted away to be replaced with miles of human flesh. When it was done, before him stood a woman, coated in the blood of a vampire, nude yet unashamed.

David gulped as her eyes flashed with scorn. "I told you to stay back," Genevieve muttered seconds before her eyes glazed over and closed, and she slid bonelessly to the floor.

Opening her eyes, Genny couldn't help but taste the sour remains of the blood on her tongue.

"Pah," she spat and hoped it would assist with removing the sensations that felt grimy.

"Dear God, I'm so pleased you've woken." A soft hand soothed her brow, a distinct contrast to the worried words.

Genevieve stretched, suddenly aware that under the scratchy thin blanket, she was naked. She stilled and looked up.

"What the actual fuck!" she snapped, her gaze connecting with David Jardin's.

"You saved my life, then collapsed." He shook his head, a grin now stretching across his face. "It was tremendous. Risky, but you were amazing."

"Great, but I need my clothes and to gather my people. Who else was injured?" Her head ached, but that really wasn't a surprise. After all, she'd been trying to ignore her inner cat for years. Successfully too, except now that it had escaped her body, she struggled with the aftereffects. It took a lot of adrenaline and energy to make the change. "I feel like someone hit me on the head, and I've passed out in the middle of an operation. So, hand me those clothes, turn around, and let me dress, and I'll get on with my job." Her voice had a scratchy tone. She detested any form of weakness, and this ranked pretty damned highly.

Without a word, her clothes were tossed over, and he turned his back.

She rose, noting the shaking of legs and arms, and cursed silently. Shrugging into her clothes, she once more demanded a status update.

"We think we've got them all. There were eleven, and one is talking. Likely because he's scared stiff." There was a hint of gaiety to the words, and she frowned.

"We don't harm or menace our suspects."

He turned, quirked an eyebrow. "No one has menaced anyone except you. Case in point." He turned to the small doorway and indicated the woman watching from beyond. Her face was pale, her entire body quavering. "She saw what you did to the vamp, and that stopped her. She's singing like a canary, in the old vernacular. Lots to tell, and we've only got some of it. She insists this is everyone who was bedding down here and looking for sanctuary from the one who made them all. Attar."

Genny's breath caught in her throat. That name once again. "And?"

"Your bear man says if I say any more, he'll gut me with a paw. Your crew is edgy. Might should get out there among the troops, let them know you're alive." His eyes glinted in the light, and she snarled.

"Fine. Whatever!"

She lurched up to him, but before she could brush past, he reached out and swiped a gentle finger over her cheek. "I'm also pleased you're okay. But I have a few questions for later."

Her eyes narrowed, and her gaze captured his. "Fine. Whatever," she repeated.

Genevieve knew she was acting like a dick. Fury at allowing the creature to emerge warred with the knowledge that she'd let the team down. All. By. Herself.

Tromping into the other room, she saw the eyes flicking in her direction. From those now gathered and restrained with what appeared to be copper chains, there was anger mixed in with a dose of starvation.

From the team, she read a mixture of relief and concern. She wanted to flick them off, treat those pesky emotions as insignificant, but they weren't that easy to shift, she knew from long experience. "I'm okay. Just a minor hiccup."

Jones—the bear man, as David had termed him—scowled. Julien frowned, and from the others, there was a tense watchfulness.

Jardin entered the room. "I've already alerted the councillor's assistant, and she's sending a secured vehicle and guards for this lot." He nodded to the assembled vampires.

"Puny human," one growled low, but the bear man simply kicked out, and that ended with the vamp howling.

The others remained silent, though certainly not cowed.

She stalked from the room and found the human contingent waiting outside. Her quick conference suggested they should check the surroundings in case any of the Rocketmen had remained, lying in wait for an attack like this.

Her skin crawled as if someone watched, and when she turned, she found Julien waiting for her.

"I need to talk to you, Genevieve."

She raised her head, her mind helpfully playing through the various insults he'd thrown at her. *Slut. Whore. Half-breed. Mutt.*

"Not at this time. We're on a job." She kept her words short and curt, hoping he'd read the hint that she wasn't interested in passing the time, let alone talking about good times past. They didn't exist. He'd wiped them out with the horrible things he'd said and done.

He winced. "I need to explain."

She whirled, the well of anguish and recriminations close to the surface.

Before she opened her mouth, David materialised in the gloom. "They're here."

His eyes searched her face, as if Jardin knew Julien had come out here in an ambush, and she couldn't think of a way to thank him without drawing attention to the fact that Julien had attempted to use this time for his own personal advantage.

Instead, she gave a curt nod, turned on her heel, and marched back inside.

CHAPTER 8

David considered himself to be a reasonably calm human, yet something about Julien Avarre rubbed him the wrong way. Maybe it was the air of condescension about him. It could have been the way he tried to bark out orders before Genevieve could speak. It was more than likely the way he watched her, like some luscious dessert there for his personal delectation.

Whatever it was, David had to restrain the urge to hit the man in his face. Right in the centre of his perfect nose.

The only positive in the mess was it was clear Genevieve wanted to do exactly the same and regularly overturned his orders.

Now that the arrests had been made, he could settle. Catch up on work he'd missed this afternoon. There were always texts and emails to field.

Looking down, he turned on the cell with the flick of a wrist.

The logo of the cell company flared along with a melodic jingle.

"You could go, if you like," she muttered, and he glanced at the woman in the front seat beside him.

Everyone else had ventured inside, but she'd seemed reluctant to follow them immediately. Anxiety washed off her like a wave. "What you saw..." Genevieve gnawed at her lower lip.

"I won't tell. But I was wondering—"

The alarm on his phone blared, and he picked it up.

The message on his cell speared him. "The nest's been attacked."

Bile, hot and sour, rose in his throat.

"What?" Her demand was tight.

"An hour ago."

She reached out a hand. "I'll come with you. Hell, move over and I'll drive."

Everything shifted to autopilot as he allowed her to steer him from the seat. Ensconced in the passenger side, he watched as she reversed in a quick sharp move, then demanded he press a button on her cell.

"Where the fuck are you going, Fernly?" Belarmino demanded.

"There's been an attack on the al bin Habbad estate. I'm escorting the *Yeux Secondes* to attend."

"*What the...?* Why didn't I know?" he bellowed.

"We've just found out, boss. I'll be in contact once I know more."

The quick exchange continued with Belarmino assuring he'd send reinforcements as soon as he could.

The whole time, David sat in the seat. Shattered.

I should have been there. He knew the dangers they all faced right now, and not to be present when those who relied on him most needed him emasculated him.

Terror coursed through his veins. He'd become invested in those who inhabited this small ecosystem of the nest, and he'd let them down. Left them without the human defences, because he'd insisted on attending the destruction of this nest.

Gutted, he sat back, running through the litany of readings and images he'd seen of previous attacks. His guts twisted into painful knots as they raced through the night.

By the time they reached the nest, groups had formed in the courtyard, mounds of bodies lay in two piles, and the injured he could see had gathered about as if they'd been triaged.

An ambulance screamed past, wailing its mournful song, heading for the big city hospital. He wondered how many others had already come and gone.

David jumped from the car before it even came to a stop, his feet taking him to the front door. Police gathered with the orange and black tape.

"You can't enter—"an officer sputtered, but quickly died away when a touch fell on David's shoulder.

He knew who it was before without looking. "Officer Fernly. He's the *Yeux Secondes*. Let him in." Genevieve's voice was low but firm, and the officer nodded.

Looking around, he saw the carnage instantly. Blood spattered the walls and floors. The scent of death was ripe on the air, and he nearly gagged. "Where? How many?"

The officer simply shook his head. "I don't know, sir. Lots. There're vamps in there." He indicated the office spaces.

Without waiting to hear more, David took off, galloping over the blood-slimed tiles while Genevieve followed.

They entered his office, and there, sitting hunched over, was Daniel, Cressida's arms enfolding him.

The couple looked up, and he saw the mix of grim acceptance and steely determination in the other man's face. Awareness bloomed. Daniel had been the *Yeux Secondes* before David. Forcing words of apology past his stiff lips didn't seem to make any difference.

"Leave us," Cressida whispered, so he backed out, thankful Genevieve hadn't entered the room behind him. The intimacy of the scene was too raw for him to remain, yet in that instant, he knew he wanted—*needed*—the same intensity of emotion.

Stepping back into the hall, he whirled to face Genevieve, her face pale. He blinked.

"I need to—"

Genevieve put her hand on his arm. "I can help. Tell me what you want, I'll do it. But first, I'll call for reinforcements."

The breath he'd held whooshed between his lips. "Thank you."

She blinked. "What? Don't thank me. There's lots to do."

He stopped her. "My timing sucks. Just... Maybe down the track..." He let the words trail away because the timing was so, so wrong.

Her eyes widened, and then she visibly clamped down on all emotions. "Later."

Genevieve moved away, raising her phone to her ear. He got the distinct impression it was a tactical retreat.

A voice called out to him, and he turned, once more assuming the role where the responsibility for the humans of the nest was his entirely. Alone.

GENEVIEVE SLUMPED ON THE STEPS. SOMEONE HAD PUSHED A BOTTLE of water into her hands, and she surveyed the now contained chaos unfolding before her.

All the injured had been triaged. Vampires were laid out in groups in the courtyard. The attackers on one side, a mound rising high towards the quickly lightening sky. The fragile human bodies had been moved to the morgue.

Whatever identification those who'd attacked had was collected so families could be apprised by the Council. They were new, fledglings, and while they'd been more than happy to murder in their frenzy, their families deserved the peace of knowing they'd found eternal rest.

The nested vampires made up a smaller pile, treated with dignity and respect as they'd attempted to defend the house.

The sun would eradicate the bodies, so only ash remained. Under normal circumstances, there would have been a memorial the next night, Genevieve knew. Not this time. There were too many issues competing.

"We'll hold a memorial later." David lowered himself to the step beside her. "This is the best we could do. The others will retreat. I'll stay. Hold a vigil so they don't go into the unknown alone."

She glanced sideways at him. "They usually burn them, don't they?"

"Some. We usually allow the sun to take the body, then memorialise the following night. This time we can't. I know some use a funeral pyre. We aren't allowed to here. Apparently it's a health hazard."

Against her will, she smiled at his dry announcement, but that small amount of mirth died away. "What happens next?"

He sighed. The sound of a wounded man. "We arrange for the mass funeral, and then we find them. Eradicate Attar and his sycophants."

She took a moment, then dropped an almost silent "I meant you."

He stilled as if she'd breached some deep, dark wall. "I can't stay here. It feels wrong, Genevieve. I want something, but it's not yet clear. This nest deserves more than I can give."

When she looked back at him, she saw he was staring off into the distance. "You're not happy being the *Yeux Secondes?*"

"Truthfully? I doubt I ever really considered that it wasn't something I didn't want to be. I was raised knowing this was where my future lay. When my parents left the House of Tudor, I stepped up, because I knew the nest and was trained. But I never fit in, not after everything that happened with Hope."

"I heard a little," Genny muttered.

His laugh was bitter. "Let me see if I can sum it up succinctly. I bought into the lies Alexa, my ex-wife, peddled, and married a woman who was a plant for the other side. Then my father fleeced the nest, and whether my mother really knew much, well, I doubt I'll ever know. They both encouraged the relationship with my wife." He hurled the words like missiles. "After Alexa was arrested, she told me the pregnancy she'd claimed was a phantom, and I divorced her. I was left feeling dirty and used. So, here I am at thirty-three, one failed marriage, one position as *Yeux Secondes* abandoned because I couldn't handle the fallout, and at the second, I've failed the house. People died because I didn't do my job."

The bitterness in his words tore at her, and she reached out. "It wasn't your fault. How could you know that—"

"I hate the job, Genevieve. In hindsight, it's not what I want to do. I'd rather live my own life on my own terms. I allowed others to direct my life, to tell me what my future was. So like a dutiful son, I let my parents dictate who I married."

He grunted and ran his hands through his hair. This time, when he looked up, there was misery in the depths of his gaze, his face tight, and his chest moved at a rapid up-and-down pace. "I had a girlfriend once, Genevieve. A long time ago. A nice girl. Sarah. She wasn't deemed suitable, and I let them pull us apart because they said I needed a wife who'd be able to assist me in running the house. The right kind with breeding." His laugh was full of self-recrimination.

"What kind of man does that make me? The only word that comes to mind is 'weak.'" He slumped now, head in his hands, between his knees. "Alexa didn't even make the cut as to breeding, yet they told me that could be overlooked because she knew her place."

Genevieve reached out without thinking and placed her hand on his shoulder while blinking tears away. He just looked dejected and defeated. Two words that never would have come to mind for this man.

"We don't have to be defined by our pasts, David. We can be more." She believed that, because it was how she attempted to live her life. She also had skeletons in her closet.

"Yeah," he muttered.

"David?"

"Yes?"

"Would you kiss me?" The words escaped before she could stop them, but once said, she wouldn't take them back or swallow them. Because she wanted that kiss with a sudden burning intensity. Wanted it with him, because that vulnerability she saw matched the one she buried deep within herself.

He looked at her, not saying a word, because the question was there in his gaze.

"I want you to kiss me." She leaned in and took his shoulder to steady herself.

They met somewhere in the middle, and the glance of flesh was soft. No more than a butterfly wing's touch, but full of promise.

When she pulled away, her heart beat a rapid tattoo. "Well..." She felt the flaming of her face but allowed a smile to curve her lips upwards. "Well," she repeated.

"Genevieve?"

"Yes, David?"

"When this is done, I want to take you out. Get to know you better."

Warmth flooded her, and she nodded. "I think I'd like that, David."

The shutters descending over the house shattered the relative silence around them. His hand snaked into hers. "Stay with me?"

His gentle request was simple to grant. "Let me send a text to the boss. I'll stay here, and when it's done, we could grab a coffee and maybe talk?"

The first rays of the sun peeked over the horizon, as golds and reds of the sunset became an absolution to those who'd attacked the nest. Sunlight traced over the garden, racing towards those who'd been lost, and with a whoosh, they ignited.

There was no birdsong as they sat and waited out the natural cremation. And when it was done, piles of ash lay in their place.

"I'll have someone come out later and clear it up." A tiny breeze wafted over them as he reached for her hand. "Come inside and we'll have that coffee."

CHAPTER 9

There'd been no time to rest, though. The House of Grimardi had also been hit. Far worse. Al bin Habbad lost many members, and Daniel's father had been just one of the dozens of victims. Grimardi fared a lot worse.

"They spread their resources," Javed growled.

"While we were dealing with one attack, they'd sent others to Grimardi. The results are catastrophic. We can take some, but two nests needing assistance? We can't help that many."

In his head, David knew the al bin Habbad nest would need to see to its own. Grimardi was in far worse condition, with over forty humans lost and ten of their warriors. His house had lost six humans, five vampires protecting the nest, and had killed thirteen of the attackers.

"Javed, I believe our numbers were less. We could take several warriors, if need be, and we can house maybe thirty of the humans in the new apartments. We haven't yet allocated them." David knew Javed was working hard to keep his anger in check. He'd been absent during the attack, and he'd felt that knowledge weighing on him.

"Indeed." The vampire steepled his fingers and glanced at David, who felt a flush creeping over his face.

Quick discussions took place, doling out the humans and vampires, finding alternative venues. Discussions continued, weighing up the pros and cons, and the whole time David felt like an outsider and intruder.

The funeral would take place the following evening, but tonight, things had to move quickly. There were too many humans and vampires left in dangerous conditions for the discussions to be prolonged.

Within the hour, the meeting broke up. Before David stood, he cleared his throat and met Javed's gaze. "Could we talk privately?"

The vampire nodded slowly. The others melted away from the room, and David waited, his emotions running riot. Once alone, Javed moved around the table so they were seated opposite.

"You have something on your mind, David?"

He nodded, trying hard to push the words out. "It's my fault. I wasn't there."

Javed waited, the silence stretching out, and David's nerves twanged with agitation.

"Javed?"

The vampire grunted, his face grave as he pushed back in his chair. "You alone are to blame?"

David stared at him. "If I'd been there, we wouldn't be in this situation."

"You have an inside working knowledge of Attar's movements? Knew they were going to attack?" His hands moved apart, palm upwards.

"Well, no."

"You can split yourself into many pieces? Fight all these vampires? Personally save and secure the nest?" The words escaped in an amused drawl.

David felt the flush, heat filling his face. "No. But—"

Javed held up a hand. "You are not to blame. You were following up on a situation. To be fair, I'm not sure why, and you were busy with the pretty officer, but you couldn't save our people. You're one man, David. But what I do sense is the question that surrounds you. You're not happy within the nest. It's different to how you've always lived, and I feel that makes you uncomfortable. Your interest in the cars and the outside forces brings many questions into play. Ones only you can answer."

David wanted to argue, but the words stuck in his throat. The truth was, as he'd told Genevieve, it wasn't right for him to be the *Yeux Secondes*. He opened his mouth to speak, but Javed shook his head.

"Now is not the time for words and decisions. It's a time to prepare, to mourn. After Attar is brought to justice, we'll talk again."

"No," David muttered. "Once this is done, I will leave. I need time to think about what I want to do. You need me to help you find a replacement. The house has already had another leave. You and yours deserve that much. But please, I haven't announced it and don't intend to. Not until Attar is dealt with."

Javed inclined his head. "Then I shall keep this to myself, but, David, you should not feel guilt. That's for those who have options. You didn't. You're a good man. One who deserves better than the hand you've been dealt."

A harsh laugh escaped. "That's funny. She said something similar too."

Javed quirked a brow. "Who?"

"Genevieve. Uh, Officer Fernly."

A smile spread across Javed's face. "Then she's a wise woman. One with demons of her own, but *Insh'Allah*," he said.

"Pardon?"

"If Allah wills it. Now, David, the night is aging, and you're in need of rest. Go. We're making plans for later."

"I should—"

Javed shook his head. "No, Cressida and Daniel are making the plans. His father and so on. Too many to count have been lost, but he's felt it harder than most. Go rest, friend." The vampire master stood and left the room without looking back.

David rose, feeling like an old man, and headed for the stairs. The scent of fresh paint, disinfectant, and cleaners assaulted his nostrils.

Rest. If only he could.

In his small room, he pulled out his cell phone and glanced down.

On a whim, he typed out a quick text. <*Wish you were here.*>

He laughed when three dots appeared on the screen straight after the delivered notification. *<Me too. Boss riding my ass. Everything ok?>*

<Yeah. See you tomorrow?>

<Maybe. Depends on what Boss says.>

<Ok. Let me know. Night.>

A tiny kiss appeared on the screen, and he couldn't control the grin. Whatever it was about Genevieve Fernly, one thing was certain: it would be really easy to get deep quickly with her.

Would that be such a bad thing? his psyche asked. With a groan, he slumped onto the bed, unable to answer his own question with certainty.

He lay still, willing his mind to settle.

Eventually he closed his eyes, and sleep came.

GENEVIEVE SLAMMED THE DOOR SHUT. “BASTARD,” SHE SNARLED. Scrunching the piece of paper in her hands, she hurled it to the other end of the room.

She didn't need to read it to remember the words. They were inscribed in her mind, like the carving on a tree trunk.

Gen, ring me. I've missed you so much and want to make it up to you. We can be great again, just give me the chance to prove it.

J

She scoffed. As if!

The focus on work should have been her key priority, but taking up a chunk of her brainpower was David Jardin, the sexy and enigmatic *Yeux Secondes*. Julien didn't count anymore. Perhaps she'd finally moved on?

She shoved the thoughts aside with a sigh.

She'd spent the last two days filling out paperwork concerning the bust on the mercantile, and another day and a bit on the attack at the nest. “And I'm not even a fucking nestling.” Not that it mattered. She'd rendered aid, had questions to answer and forms to fill in.

It was always the way of things in the service.

She sipped her coffee and settled at the table, her eyes half closed as she rested. The nights had been long, the days longer, and her rest almost non-existent.

Even as she slipped into a twilight type trance, the phone rang.

"Hello?"

"Genny?" Julien's voice filtered over the line, and she almost growled.

"What do you want?"

"Another chance, *petite*. I know I hurt you—"

Now she laughed, the sound dark and filled with malice. "*Really*? When did you work that one out? Stop calling me. No more notes, Julien. We're done." She hung up, then stared at the phone as if it were a poisonous snake. "Enough!" She reached out, ready to dial a number, then snarled, grabbed her keys and purse. She needed air and a run. Nothing less would soothe her right now.

At the door, realisation bloomed. The funeral was tonight. He surely wouldn't welcome her intrusion. Even so, there was the urgency to check on him thrumming in her veins. It was more than intention and need. It was... more a compulsion, Genny admitted.

Dropping the keys and purse on the table by the door, she headed for the bathroom. A shower would help, then maybe sleep. She dropped the cell on the bed as she moved towards the bathroom, stripping as she went. Her uniforms lying by the hamper reminded her that laundry was well overdue too.

The water from the shower ran hot, and she slid beneath it, letting it wash away the fatigue and frustration. Soaping and rinsing her hair took only moments, and she considered briefly cutting it short.

None of the girls in the pride did that. It was like some kind of unwritten rule, Genny guessed.

"Maybe it's time," she muttered, turning the water off and stepping onto the mat while wrapping the towel around herself. Peering into the fogged mirror, the strands hanging down, her gaze moved to the red mark on her chest. The daily reminder of the past she couldn't outrun.

Genny grabbed the hank of hair and held it away, imagining it short. Her face was slight, and the curl bouncing up framed it. "Hmm, shows promise."

Dropping her towel, she bent and started sorting through the laundry. One thing her mother had been insistent on when she bought her apartment was her own washing machine. Her mother's words reminding her that this way only *her* underwear went in it, not the multitude of others' living in the complex, had stuck. Of course, that hadn't been the only thing she'd thrown a fit about when Genny moved in.

Genny had never been happier than today though, as she hung her clothes on the small drying rack suspended above the washer and let them hang in her own time. "Saves on ironing," she reminded herself.

Once satisfied she'd done all she could, Genny moved back to the bedroom, seeking something to wear and settling on a pair of black, lightly heeled boots paired with a plain white blouse and black jacket with three-quarter sleeves and slim-fit jeans. Her hair, secured into a loose knot held with a clip, completed the look. A quick glance in the mirror assured her it was sombre enough and wouldn't stand out against the sea of vampires and nestlings.

Even as Genny snatched up the keys, her cell rang, and without looking, she pressed the Answer button, hoping it wasn't work. "Genevieve Fernly."

"Genevieve, will you be there?" David's voice flowed down the line, and flickers of lust danced through her nerve endings.

"I'm leaving now."

"Good. I'll meet you outside."

She shook her head. "No, you should be in a seat. I'll find you."

He huffed but hung up.

Warmth spread through her belly at the knowledge that he'd wait for her. It was a new and untested emotion, but one that came with a dollop of hope.

She raced for her compact gold-flecked car.

CHAPTER 10

David kept his eye on the door, willing Genevieve to arrive. She did and slid into the seat beside him, panting. "Sorry, traffic was a snarl, then finding somewhere to park."

He handed her the order of service, hands glancing together, and a frisson of awareness spread through his body. *What is it about this woman?*

"Just glad you made it." Their gazes connected, long seconds passed, and then he glanced away.

The funeral was sombre, with so many lost from the local nest. Then they'd included the memorial for those lost in New Orleans as well, given the houses in Louisiana had indicated there was more than they could handle in one go. Houses were like families. Mass funerals, though not a regular occurrence, meant single ceremonies were not welcomed in these circumstances.

When it was over, those gathered moved out onto the lawn. No traditional wake would be held, though individuals may gather in their friendship groups. Tonight, David needed the company of Genevieve.

Once it was done, he excused himself for a moment and approached Kharisma. "Can you take control for the evening?" He'd struck up a healthy working relationship with Javed's second. He trusted her and expected nothing more to occur this evening. Not with so many other vampires in attendance.

Her eyebrow arched. "Going somewhere?"

He nodded. "Yes."

Her interest wasn't quashed by his single-word answer. "It's personal," he added.

"Then of course. You will return before sunrise?"

"I would expect so," he muttered. Truthfully, he didn't know, but it was the only answer he could give honestly.

THEY SETTLED INTO THE CAR, AND GENEVIEVE DROVE THEM INTO town. "So, I didn't organise anything special." She felt anxiety gnawing at her but refused to let her disquiet show.

"No. That's fine. Perhaps we should stop, have a drink somewhere quiet?"

She nodded and kept her gaze on the road until she reached the outskirts of town, then pulled into a parking bay. "I, um... Sometimes I come here."

The bar was quiet when they entered, and they took a seat in a secluded corner, the velvet of the booth dipping down beneath their combined weight.

A server came over, took their order, and then they sat there as the silence stretched between them. Awkward and unforgiving.

The drinks were delivered, and Genny was pleased to have something to do with her hands.

"So... you do this often?" She glanced down, uncomfortable and wondering what his answer might be.

His bark of laughter had her looking up with surprise. "I'm new back on the market, Genevieve. I was married."

She nodded, feeling ridiculous, and looked down at the hand he slid onto the tabletop before her. "God, such a stupid question."

David squeezed her hand. "No. You're nervous. I'm nervous. We're in uncharted waters here, and starting a conversation can be difficult."

Genny sighed. "It's tough. I mean, it's been years since I was involved with anyone, and the last time it didn't work out so well."

"Then let's keep it light, shall we?" He released her hand. "To friends." David raised his glass, took a sip. "Not bad," he murmured.

"I found out about this place accidentally when I moved here. They've got some good wines." She shrugged. "Not that I drink much. You do things when you lose your inhibitions."

"There's not much chance of that in the houses. Or at least the one I grew up in."

Genny raised a brow. "It can't have been that bad. The House of Tudor is a settled nest of long standing."

He shook his head. "It's really all smoke and mirrors. Truly, I didn't realise how... *stifling* and miserable I was until I left. The *Yeux Secondes* is supposed to be the master's second eyes, the human equivalent of the vampire second. My father took advantage of the position for his own gains. I did as I was told and was the obedient son. Dutiful but blind to what was happening, and I swallowed the lies I was fed. Hope broke away, and I learned the hard way that everything you think is perfect isn't always what it appears from the outside."

Genny bit her lip. "But you've learned."

"Yes, but at cost. My relationship with Hope is improving, but it likely will never be close. My parents... If I never see them again, it will be enough. But enough about my misery. Tonight, I want to know more about you."

Genevieve frowned. "I'm an open book. A mutt—"

"Stop," David growled, anger infusing the word.

"What?"

"Never call yourself that again, Genevieve. You're a woman. A beautiful, strong woman who has committed her life to society." Passion oozed from him, and she wanted to stop him but controlled that instinct.

Genevieve blushed and unconsciously raised her hands to her burning cheeks. "I..."

"Please, Genny."

The soft words turned her insides to mush.

"I'll try. For you." The smile he turned on her was like a million light globes, bright and full of hope. She blinked rapidly. "We should order," she muttered, glancing down to the menu beside her drink.

As if he understood her nervousness, he changed topics to the food on offer, though really any kind of contemplation was like trawling through molasses. What she ordered in the end, Genny couldn't say, but she squirmed as heat battered her insides.

"So, brothers? Sisters?"

Raising her head, the seed of an idea bloomed. "I have half-siblings, Syrah and Franc along with a brother—twin— Bastien. He's found a life partner, and I wonder... *Wouldyoucomewithme?*" The words tumbled from her mouth in a rush.

Now it was his turn to appear lost for words. "I... uh..."

"Never mind." She ducked her head as embarrassment crashed down on her.

When David reached out and touched a hand to her chin, it was to tug her face up and keep it there so their gazes melded. "That's not a no, Genny. I'm just surprised you'd ask me."

It was the hint of vulnerability that tore at her.

"What? Why not you?"

He laughed, the sound harsh and jarring. "I'm not exactly a prince, you know. I'm a human, a failed *Yeux Secondes* of one and soon to be two nests, and divorced. Not exactly a prize to warm any mother's heart."

For a moment she considered the scouring assessment. "Being human in a world so topsy-turvy is maybe more of a positive than not, David." Before any other words could escape though, the server arrived with their meals.

They ate in silence, gazes catching and holding for long moments while her belly jounced and tickled, arousal winding her tighter than a piano wire. Pulling away from those drugging connections grew harder each time. Finally, unable to complete her dinner, she scooted back. "I'm going..." She indicated to the restroom with her thumb.

He must have read her inner turmoil on her face, because he shook his head, his eyes glinting with promise as he waved to the server. "Check, please."

The air between them crackled with a sensual intensity.

He dragged notes from his wallet while the server collected the bill, then threw them on the salver. "Keep the change."

From the look on the woman's face, clearly it was a lot, but David reached for Genny's elbow and steered her from the restaurant at a rapid clip.

"You drive," he demanded, his face drawn tight, and heat reached out to her from his gaze.

They climbed into the car, and for a moment, it was as if all the air in the cabin was sucked out. The rapid thrum of her heart echoed loudly enough that she was sure he could hear it. Arousal had never been so overwhelming before.

Or maybe she'd just never met a man who made her *feel* like this. She exhaled and turned the key she'd shoved into the ignition.

By unspoken agreement, the ride was silent. No radio or discussion, just the sound of the wheels and their breathing to wind around them both. Like they'd somehow moved beyond the everyday cares of the world and had their own private bubble.

She bit her lip as she drove into the parking zone and stopped at her allocated area.

They climbed from the car, and their eyes met across the top of the vehicle. She nodded, agreeing with the unspoken question of "Are you sure?"

They met at the front of the car. He took her hand, and she led the way up the stairs to her building. It was compact, older, built decades earlier, and for a moment, she wondered what he'd think of her most private space.

She'd chosen the location on the outskirts of town because of the access to green space.

"It's..." She shrugged. "It's mine. I bought it a couple years ago. I've done work—"

"Shhh." He stepped up, took her shoulders, his hands moulding over them. Then leaned in, so slowly and achingly. His lips touched hers.

She sighed as the tension that had filled her entire being suddenly floated away. "David..."

His finger slid over her lips, silencing whatever she'd planned to say. "I want to be with you, Genny. But only if you're ready."

Tears burned, and she managed a smile. "I am. I want you too, David."

"Then let me inside." The double entendre broke through the last fleeting threads of her anxiety.

With a quick move, she inserted and turned the key, opened the door.

She barely had time to close it when he tugged her close, kissed her again with searing passion, lips and hands urging her body to quake in response.

Unable to think, she tugged at his tie, needing to wrench it away so she could unbutton his shirt.

Movements were urgent and jerky as she feasted on his lips. He tugged back, his tongue laving the skin of her neck, and she arched. "David..."

"Let me touch you, Genny." The pop of a button, the ragged sigh as cotton tore, and the urgent zip rasping was all that was left while their desire drove them forwards.

"Please," she whispered as he pushed her pants from her legs, taking her panties with them. A whisper of cool air caressed her body. *Naked.*

She opened her beleaguered eyes that she'd closed during the wild, passionate undressing.

David was standing there, not a stitch of clothing covering his body, and she couldn't control the sigh of pleasure that escaped her lips. "You're beautiful, David."

He laughed. "Not so much of that." His smile melted as the heat grew in his gaze once more.

It washed over her, a wave of erotic hunger she couldn't deny, because inside she felt its twin growing, unfurling and demanding.

Skin brushed against skin. She sucked in an unsteady breath and grabbed his hard biceps, heat scorching her palms as she moaned with delicious anticipation while his cock drove into her belly.

"I want you, Genny," he said with a growl. "You're a beautiful woman."

The words echoed through her bones, and she shivered. "Come."

They flowed to the bedroom, hands entwined, letting the moment swell around them. When his mouth crashed upon hers, the hunger and yearning demanded everything.

The mating of lips and tongue, thrust and parry, filled her mind while his hands wove magic over her skin.

They crashed down to the bed, and she welcomed him by winding her legs around him. He moved with her, accepting the embrace, surging deep within her body in a single thrust.

He grunted. "Genny?"

"More," she demanded.

The wild undulations and moves sped up until she couldn't tell where she ended and he began, lost in the maelstrom while her mind whirled madly. Sensations chased away thought, and she just felt.

Her fingers skated over slick skin. Nails bit deep. Sighs filled the air along with the scent of musk.

Genny's body was tighter than wire before she fell and they moved together in an erotic rhythm only they heard. Down she dropped. Deep into the well of pleasure until the very edge of reality broke away, shattered. Eyes blinded by the demands of a wild orgasm, she held on, rode the waves until she slumped back, exhausted.

David was still moving, faster and wilder, until he too reached the point of fulfilment. Suddenly he slumped over her, perspiration-drenched, soft and weighty.

Her chest bellowed as she fought for breath, but the long fingers of slumber reached out and tore her awareness away, and she drifted off.

CHAPTER 11

David lay there, looking up at the ceiling while the woman cuddled up beside him snored in a delightfully soft manner.

The sex—he refused to consider it lovemaking—had been cataclysmic and a revelation. It had been deep. Meaningful.

Genevieve differed from any other woman he'd ever met. He could, he supposed, put it down to her nature. Volatile yet controlled. Brief flashes of emotional depth and dark emotions before they once again were replaced with her affable front. Perhaps a ploy to keep people far away from the fragile woman he's spied beneath the surface? She was a complex being.

It wasn't just her genetic make-up either. She might have been a shifter, but he'd had enough interactions with them over the years to know they were as human in affairs of the heart as he was. They may have fiery depths, but he knew they shied away from such interactions with regular humans due to the difficulties of explaining that they might assume animal form while lost in passion. But for all that, he knew they were more humane than many humans.

What she showed was indefinable and scary by equal measure. A passion that was honest. Consuming.

What do I do? His question to the universe remained unanswered.

He wanted to know more, and definitely another opportunity to be with this woman, but with so much at stake, was she the right woman at the right time? Was he simply jumping into a situation because he needed that emotional connection?

Long moments passed while she slept, and he wrestled with his fears. Time that rolled ever forwards while he stagnated, lost in the mire of his own emotions.

With careful moves, he extricated himself and snatched up his clothes where he'd scattered them on the floor. Averting his gaze from the woman on the bed, he slipped his clothes on over his cooling body. David prowled the tiny unit while his confusion roiled inside.

He reached for the door and let himself out.

GENEVIEVE WOKE. THE APARTMENT *FELT* EMPTY. HER NAKEDNESS revealed that what had happened wasn't a dream.

"David?" Her soft call had no answer. She rose and grabbed for a robe, wound it around herself, and padded into the kitchen. Empty. Just as she'd feared.

Shame washed over her, a burning wave.

She'd allowed him in. Taken a chance. But in the end, here she was, alone. A sob filled her throat. "No. Don't go there," she told herself.

Fury and fear rose in equal measure. Bones snapped and claws popped free, replacing her fingernails. The animal within was rising, needing release along with her ragged emotions.

"I will not let the animal take me." Genny panted and fought the creature inside herself, pain radiating through her as she forced the animal back. Buried it once more, though she knew her control was worn thin. "I'll have to let it out soon."

The words echoed in the empty room, and she closed her burning eyes. "What the hell is it about me that's so fucking unlovable? Why is there no one who can accept me as I am?"

Tears burned as she turned to the kettle. Coffee would help, she told herself. It was that or alcohol, and a swift look at the clock reminded her she'd be on the clock again in a few hours.

She ground beans, heated the water, and had just prepared the plunger when a knock echoed. With a frown, she walked to the door and wrenched it open.

David stood on the other side, misery and confusion filling his eyes. "I had to go for a walk."

She held the door open. "What do you want?" The question sprang free, highlighting the fears she couldn't escape. For a moment she wondered if he could see the hurt he'd inflicted by leaving, but in the next heartbeat, she banished that thought. *Don't go there.*

"Can I come in?" A jagged crack of lightning filled the darkness, so he shone in the oppressive black of night.

She stepped back. Allowed him in.

You're making a mistake, her psyche warned.

Or taking the greatest chance of your life, added her heart.

"I needed to think clearly, but I wasn't leaving." He reached out, fingers curling softly against her cheek.

She jerked away, and his lips thinned.

He reached again, cupped Genevieve's cheek, and she sighed and leaned in to the caress while the ache in her chest eased.

"I thought you'd gone," she whispered before realising she'd said the words aloud.

The fire in his eyes softened. "No, Genevieve, I wouldn't leave like that." He kicked the door shut. "You deserve better than that." He sniffed the air, as if sensing how close to the edge she skated. "Coffee?"

She shrugged and headed to the kitchen, silently dragged another cup from the cupboard, and plunged the coffee, grateful for a moment or two where she could hide and regroup.

He read the rejection in her eyes. Genevieve thought he'd left, and he cursed himself for not realising just how much his thoughtlessness had cost. *Ham-handed fool.* Nothing had prepared him for the guilt that now coursed through him.

"I'm sorry, Genevieve. I shouldn't have left without telling you. I just needed air."

She shook her head. "No. It's fine. No promises were made, after all."

"But I need to explain—"

She turned, thrust the coffee at him. "No you don't. I understand."

He winced at the blank look on her face. On a sigh, he shoved the mug to the bench beside he, and cupped her face. Gazed deeply, hoping she'd read the honesty there. "I needed to think. This whole situation has taken me by surprise, and I don't know how to deal with it."

She blinked.

"Genevieve, I feel something for you. It's big and it's scary, and I don't know if I can trust it because I wasn't a good pick last time. So I went outside, hoping some fresh air would clear my brain. I meant to be back before you woke, because I had no intentions of leaving. Unless you want me gone?"

The slow blink was joined by a shake of her head. "No," she whispered. "But I woke to silence. If I'd known..." She shrugged. "Everyone else has left me when things get tough, but I didn't expect it this time." Genevieve slid a shaking hand over her mouth. "I didn't mean to say all that."

He pulled her close, so their foreheads touched, and sighed. "Probably not, but thank you for sharing it with me. It means a lot."

"I'm a loser," she muttered.

Now David tugged back. "Not at all, Genevieve. It means you've been hurt, and I should be more careful of your feelings."

The bark of laughter was wet. "I'm not a china doll, David."

"No you're not." But gazing into her eyes, he knew she was far more fragile than she let on, and he felt the responsibility to protect her heart in the future.

He weighed up her reaction and decided the best defence right now was to be firm. "Come on." He lifted the coffee and reached for her hand. "Come back to bed."

She opened her mouth, and he shook his head. "We can talk or cuddle or anything you want, Genevieve. Just tell me what you need."

"I don't know."

He believed her, because her eyes were wide and startled, pulse jumping at her throat, betraying her.

"We can take this as slow as you want or need."

She took his hand, the touch like the wing of a nervous bird, shaking and shivering, and reached for her coffee. "Okay."

CHAPTER 12

Early morning brought with it an additional layer of uncertainty, and Genny wasn't really sure how to handle it.

David had roused her by sliding his hand over her shoulder, and she stretched and purred. "I need to get back to the house before dawn. Can you take me, or I should I grab a cab?"

Genny opened her eyes, peered at the clock: 4:00 a.m. "No, I can take you. Just give me a moment to dress."

Before she could rise though, David took her in his arms. "Not before I wish you good morning." Then he did so, with a thoroughness that left her breathless and hot.

"David?" she whispered as he pulled away.

"I really wish we had time to continue this, but I have to get back." He frowned and ran an unsteady hand through his hair, and for the first time, Genny was aware he was once more fully dressed. When they'd finally settled in for the night, he'd worn nothing, and the memory of bare skin against bare skin had her swallowing while her body reacted with goosebumps.

He groaned. "I really don't have time..."

She grinned. "I'm just teasing."

"I know," he growled, and she laughed.

"Come to the house. Stay the night with me."

She blinked.

"Please."

In his gaze, she read both earnestness and uncertainty. His damned ex-wife had been a prize, she thought. A real class-A bitch. "I'll try. It depends on the day, though. If I can, I will, David."

He nodded with a quick jerk of his head. "Okay."

Genevieve sprang out of the bed, opened the drawers where she'd stashed her newly clean underwear, and hurried through dressing, her body more than a little aware of her audience. As the brush of her bra over sensitized nipples or the slight tug of panties over already swollen intimate zones heightened her arousal, she tried really hard to ignore the pull.

Finally, she tamed her hair, then hurried to the bathroom to run a brush over her teeth before sliding into her boots.

"Ready," she called, going into the kitchen to see him putting the final touches on to-go cups of coffee.

"Here." He thrust one into her hands. "I know you like a cup."

Such a simple act, but it touched her deeply. Moisture burned behind her eyelids, but she blinked it away. "We should get moving." As they moved to the door, she snatched up her small bag containing ID, purse, and gun, then grabbed her keys.

She closed the door, and for a moment, it felt like she'd done something momentous. The act became a portent, but she snorted silently and thrust the idea away. *No building castles and picket fences, girl.* She'd done that before, and look where she'd ended up.

Once in the car, she took a long deep swallow. "Won't there be questions if I join you tonight?"

His smile was warm. "No, there was an invitation extended for you, Genevieve." He reached out and slipped a wayward strand of hair behind an ear. "I won't push, but I'd like you to join me."

She slid the cup into the drink holder, started the car, and smoothly drove out onto the road. Traffic was light, but she remained quiet, figuring if she didn't know what to say, silence would be best.

As if he understood, David didn't speak until they reached the steps.

"Think about it. Let me know your decision." Then he leaned in with a quick, hard kiss before hurrying out and up the steps.

THE DAY DRAGGED. BY LUNCHTIME, THOUGH DAVID HAD BEEN mired in reconstruction plans, checking amendments to the new structures, and attending to issues with the business, he'd already looked at the clock a million times.

He drank deeply of the coffee, rubbed his eyes, and turned to the next pile of urgent tasks.

By mid-afternoon, with no news from Genevieve, he scowled.

When the cell phone rang, he answered it.

"Sorry I haven't called. We've had a bit of a situation down here to sort out. I don't know what time—" She sounded winded, and he frowned, wondering what had happened.

His hand squeezed the phone. "Doesn't matter the time. Whenever, because you're always welcome here, Genevieve."

"David, I have to go. There's..." Shouts echoed, and she sighed. "I have to go, but I'll be there as soon as I can."

"I'll be waiting," he countered. Then she disconnected so all he could hear was the tone on the line.

GENEVIEVE'S LIPS THINNED AS SHE WATCHED THE MAN BEING LOADED into the cell. The call with David had been short, but she'd desperately needed to hear his voice.

The day had turned out to be a real disappointment.

Her contact turned up dead in a back alley. Dried up and hacked to pieces, literally.

They'd gotten wind of a planned influx of bikers who were angry disaffected shifters. Looking for trouble, and more than one psychotic member with a grudge against the Liaison Division.

The Attar situation was biting too, with the city government unhappy that the trouble had come to town, and why hadn't the

Liaison Division done more to curb the situation? The boss had to meet with the mayor and came back looking more like a bull with a sore head.

Now this.

"I'll get you, bitch!" The angry selkie's tones filled the silence.

With a sigh, she sat down to write out her report when the boss came stalking in.

"Got him?"

She nodded. "Yeah."

He cocked an eye. "Not before he got a few licks in."

He didn't need to remind her. The blow from a meaty hand had made contact with her eye and ribs.

"You look like you should go home, get some rest and heal." His gaze fluttered over her face. She knew the reddish purple around her eye was off-putting.

"Soon. Once the report is finished. I've already sent the nymph home. Her information about what she'd seen and where to find the pelt proved quite useful."

"Just a shame your partner is off sick." Boss's eyes bulged as he spoke, and Genny knew he was less than pleased that the human she'd been working with was once again absent.

"I don't think the Liaison Division is quite what he thought it would be."

The man opposite laughed. The bullhorn-like sound never ceased to surprise her. "Yes. He's put in his retirement paperwork."

She nodded, licking her lips. "He'd said he planned to. Anyway, I do prefer to work alone."

"You need backup, Genevieve. Just like the rest of us. Your inner creature is powerful, but one day, you'll find someone stronger. I don't leave my people to face challenges greater than their strength."

She grimaced and rubbed an aching rib. "Yeah, I know. I'll finish this, and then I'm gone."

He grunted, rose, then turned back to pin her with a glare. "You're going home?"

Had he read something in her eyes today? "No. I'm... I'm going to be off-site tonight."

"Be careful, Genevieve. There's too many potholes around right now to get lost."

She bit her lip, more than aware of that. When he left, she turned back to her screen and tapped slowly, wanting the thing done so she could honestly settle in for a night of... what? "Just what do I expect?"

The problem, as far as Genny could see, was that there was no obvious answer. Sure, she wanted the sex. Who wouldn't? The closeness of another living being was also a component of the decision-making process. The C-word loomed in the back of her mind, scary and growing ever more demanding.

Shaking her head, Genny sighed. The words on the screen were little more than a mass of letters. No sense in what she'd written. "This is getting in the way of my life," she huffed indignantly.

Backspacing, Genny deleted the gobbledegook and pondered her words, describing the altercation that took place. The human who'd been dragged back in a fugue state wouldn't remember, thankfully. Selkies' mind control was pretty damn strong, given they would drown their prey, and it was only because she held the skin that she was able to control it. That didn't mean it wasn't furiously angry, though.

Sliding her head down to the desk eased some of the thudding ache from her skull, but there was still much to do. The precinct's medical officer had raised a concern of concussion, but she'd waved them away.

It wasn't like she had a viable partner now.

"Fernly, is that report finished?" The disembodied voice of the boss rang out, and she sighed.

"Nearly." If she were diligent, it could be completed in the next ten minutes.

She fought the bloom of pain in her head, finished the report, hit Send, and leaned back in her seat, eyes closed.

"One of the team will drive you home." His voice boomed by her side, and she opened her eyes.

"I was going to al bin Habbad."

Silence stretched between them.

"Home," he finally growled, and she gave up, rising and absorbing the hiss that wanted to escape between her lips.

It was only once she was in the shower that she realised she hadn't yet contacted David. How would he react? Would he be pissed that she hadn't told him the boss had sent her home? Would he worry?

Not that he should. She'd been alone for a long time and had faced far more dangerous situations than this before.

"I can look after myself," she muttered as the water sluiced down her body.

But no matter what she might think, it would be wrong to leave him hanging. So once she'd stepped from the shower and dried off, she settled into the bed, snatched up the cell, and sent a message to David.

<Can't make it tonight. Stuff happened and I'm at home. I'll contact you tomorrow.>

Slumping back against the pillow, she closed her eyes, drifting off.

SOMETIME LATER, A BANGING AT HER DOOR ROUSED HER, AND SHE rolled to the edge, dropping from the bed, head pounding in time with the echo of the door.

"I'm coming," she muttered, dragging the wrap around her nude body and moving slowly.

She peered through the peephole.

David. Pissed, face tight, and eyes spitting fire.

She opened the door.

"What the...?" He stepped up, gripping her chin hard. "What the fuck happened to you?" He didn't stay still long enough to hear her answer before scooping her up and slamming the door behind him.

RAGE ROSE IN A BOILING MASS FROM BELLY TO GULLET. ONE EYE swollen and radiating tones of purple and red while the rest of her face was pale, and the grunt of pain she gave when he picked her up had his pulse racing.

"Who the fuck hurt you?"

Her eye, the one not swollen almost completely shut, widened. "It was a work thing."

Pushing through to the bedroom, he lowered her to the coverlet, then reached for the knotted belt of her wrap.

Genevieve batted at his hands ineffectually. "What are you doing?"

He ground his teeth together at the pain threading through her tone. "I need to see how bad the damage is, damn it!" Control was a thin thread, almost ready to crack under the pressure of the fear riding him.

"I'm okay. Really."

"Bullshit! You're pale, one eye almost shut, and that sound you gave when I picked you up says it's not the only injury. You should be in hospital. Why didn't you ring me?" The last words were little more than a hiss. They betrayed the true level of his anxiety, but he clearly didn't care.

Her hands stilled him, warm and curving over his fingers. "I'm okay, David. I've seen the medic."

"And they let you come home. No one to watch over you. That's not good enough." Truly, if he'd been able to get hold of the medic right now, he'd likely squeeze them dry. *She should have come to me.*

"I wanted to come home. We're not..." She waved one hand in the air. "There's no actual agreement between us, David. I mean, one night of awesome sex—"

His fury notched up. "Sex? You think that's all this is?" He realised exactly what he'd said, but the words were out. Spoken. He wasn't the kind of guy who'd recant on the truth, though. It told him his emotions were engaged in a level he'd never before felt. The terror that shot through him when he'd gotten the text still rippled through his nerve endings, and seeing her, the way she moved carefully, the pallor of her features, the reality of the shiner? They all built up to something he couldn't deny. Terror he might have lost her and never known.

"Damn it, Genevieve, I was worried."

She blinked. "Come on, David. It's a work thing."

Clearly she didn't realise just how deep the effect of seeing her in this condition; otherwise, she wouldn't have uttered the words. "Bullshit, Genevieve. I don't care if you think I'm some kind of idiot." His ire rose, scalding him.

"I don't think you're an idiot—" she began.

"Really? So, it didn't occur to you that I was waiting for you. Then I get this text." He shoved the cell in her direction. "After last night..." He traced angry circles on the carpet of her bedroom floor, shoving his hands through his hair because he needed to control the terror that continued to shoot right through his gut. David turned, speared her with his gaze. "I'm in deep, Genevieve. I told you that just this morning in the kitchen. But the thought that, for all that, you won't take even the most basic of steps to protect yourself—"

"What? No!" Her bellow didn't ease the greasy waves swamping him.

"Of course it is. Or is it you just don't care about how others see you? How I see you? That text nearly killed me, Genevieve. I was in the office when it came through, and I left in the middle of the nightly handover. That's how much I was worried. Terrified."

Her mouth hung open, as if none of this had occurred to her, and for a moment—a long wild moment—he wondered if that were truly the case. But he was burning. The emotions incendiary. He stalked forwards and bent down. "I was beside myself, Genevieve." Tears pricked his eyes.

"I'm sorry," she whispered. "I didn't realise because I've been alone for too long, David, and it didn't occur to me—" Her words broke off. "I didn't mean to hurt you. I just didn't think."

The words slaughtered him, because he could read it was exactly what she felt. That she'd not needed to tell anyone because no one cared.

He closed his eyes. Inhaled as he fought to control his emotions. The touch of her hand had them flashing open again.

"Please promise me, Genevieve, you'll always let me know when you're hurt." It wasn't nearly enough to soothe him, but it was a first step, and he let the racing of his heart settle when she nodded.

"I will. I'm really sorry though, David. Please."

He sighed and bent down. Gathered her close and let himself inhale the scent of her.

It would do. For now.

CHAPTER 13

Waking, Genevieve opened her eyes and groaned. As a shifter hybrid, she had some acceleration to healing, but it only truly kicked in if she allowed herself to change.

Yet another reason to hate the abomination she was.

The sound of footsteps had her looking to the doorway. David was there suddenly, mug in hand. "Thought you'd woken. I brought you a coffee."

He looked like he should have been zoned out on the bed, with a cheeky stubble shading his jaw and bruises under his eyes.

"What... what time is it?"

"It's 10:00 a.m."

She heard the words, her guts freezing. Then she moved, but the tug of pain in her ribs and the wave of pain rattling her brain had her subsiding with a groan.

"Back against the pillows, slugger," he murmured, advancing until he stood at her side of the bed. He sat and the mattress dipped, rolling her a little closer. "How are you feeling?"

"Stupid. I'm meant to be at work." She pinned him with a glare. "Pass me my phone so—"

"Nuh-uh." He held it up. "Your boss rang. I explained you were resting and about your injuries. He's pissed you didn't disclose them all, and as of now, you're on medical leave until you've been deemed able to return to work."

"Medical leave? Who the hell gave you the right—" She stopped and raised her hand to her throbbing brow.

"You were out of it when the cell rang. Then the text said if you didn't answer, they'd break down your door." He held up the screen so she could see it.

"Argh!"

"Now you have two choices. You stay here, and I end up taking leave so I can look after you, or you come back to the nest with me. There you have access to 24/7 medical care, meals on tap, and I can monitor you."

She narrowed her eyes. "How about neither?" she hissed. Oh yes, she was misbehaving, but steamrolling wasn't something she took well.

He smiled and shook his head. "One or the other, and those are your two options."

Genevieve balled her fists. He had assumed an implacable will, and she doubted she'd win. But the option of being cared for was tempting.

"So which choice, Genevieve? I need to let people know too."

Not that he was trying to guilt her, but she knew he had responsibility for so many others. So why add her to the list? She bit the words down before they could escape. "Fine. We'll go. Just so you won't be worrying about everyone else."

David's brow furrowed. "Genevieve, you're important. That's why I came."

She sniffed back the sudden weak tears that scorched her eyes. "Yeah. I hear you. I need to get up. Dressed. Pack some clothes."

"I'll pack for you. You only need comfortable stuff, and I already found your suitcase. It's in the lounge, ready."

She blinked. "You were so sure—"

"Hopeful." He framed her face with a soft hand. "Please. I know you're uncomfortable with this, but right now, it's better if I'm at the nest."

"Sure." She let him take her hand and help her from the bed, though the movement still had pain blooming. "Clothes."

He scooped up the pile she didn't remember leaving on the chest of drawers. "You do what you need to. I'll be just outside if you need me."

Alone in the room once he'd left her, she shuffled for the bathroom, eyed the shower, but ignored it. Her toiletries bag lay on the counter, toothbrush and paste balancing on the top.

Within minutes, she was dressed. She carried the bag from the bathroom and handed it to David, who stashed it among piles of track pants, panties, and soft shirts. Not a bra in sight. But then, she wasn't wearing one now, either. The band had posed far too much pressure against her bruised ribs.

She shrugged. A problem for another day.

He fastened the suitcase, and had her out the door before she could say a word. The car waiting was dark and boxy. One she'd been in previously, with room to manoeuvre in the seat.

The trip passed in silence. As they drew up to the front steps, a woman waited, took the keys from his hands once he'd seen her safely from her seat and the suitcase was once more in his hands. She carried the small bag he'd already stashed in the car before she'd left the apartment. It was filled with her small laptop, purse, keys, cell, and some books. He planned to keep her busy, by the looks of it.

He ushered her into a small seating area. "Grab a book. I'll be a little while. When I'm done, I'll take you up to the bedroom. There's a private bathroom, and I'll have lunch brought up."

He handed the suitcase off to a hovering team and disappeared into another room.

She levered herself down to the chair, dragged a book from the bag, and sighed, settling in for who knew how long.

DAVID WORKED FEVERISHLY OVER THE NEXT SEVERAL DAYS, AWARE that within the safety of the nest, Genevieve was healing. Chafing, it was true, because he refused to allow her to do anything other than rest. Each day she was examined to ascertain how close she was to healed, and he was aware time was ticking away. Shifter healing was quick, and if the report he'd received today was anything to go by, he'd have to let her return home tomorrow so she could assume her duties.

A knock echoed, and he raised his head from signing off on the work orders littering his desk. "Come."

He must have jerked with surprise, because the hulking man who now stood in his office smiled.

Before now, David had the impression of a large, meaty man with blunt features and sharp eyes. Today, he couldn't miss the breadth of the shoulders or the danger that emanated in waves. "Ah, Lieutenant. Take a seat."

He shook his head. "No. But I am checking in on Genevieve. We need her back as soon as she's able, but if I asked her, she'd have returned the same day." The man cocked his head. "You have a vested interest, and after you contacted me with her whereabouts, I knew she'd be in the best care."

David settled back in his seat. "She's healing well, but yes, you're right. If she'd been able, she'd have returned by the afternoon after. Genevieve doesn't tend to put her own interests first, so someone had to do it for her."

"Agreed," the man growled.

"She will return tomorrow, but I'm concerned that she's working alone."

The man's eyes quirked. "She told you that?"

"And that her current partner is retiring."

Now the man lowered himself into a large armed chair, which squeaked as he allowed it to cradle his bulk. "Yes, that's all true. You looking to take the role on?" That gaze pinned him, as if attempting to extract truths David had no idea he held.

David started. Then he shifted in his chair. He'd never considered that as an option. "I might," he prevaricated, because that thought was worming its way down inside him. Lodging where it would likely take root, David thought with shock.

The man grunted. "You'd be a welcome asset, to be honest. We don't have much call for interaction with vamps, or at least until now we haven't, but things are changing, David. Shifters and fairies and the others, we're not quite a dime a dozen, but vamps are funny. Remote, but in the last couple years, things have changed, and not for the better. There's unrest between humans and vamps and others of the para world. We could do with insight."

David nodded. "All true, but that's how they've evolved. Outside the world and apart, but with their own rules and regulations. Without too much interaction with the others until, as you said, now."

"When your time here"—he indicated to the house—"is done, talk to me." He rose. "Bring her tomorrow. We could do with your insight. Stuff's going down, not related to this whole Attar rubbish but other stuff. Shifters are on edge, as is everyone. We've got a new problem, and I think you might be able to explain some things."

David frowned. "I can take a look now—"

But even as he spoke, the man left the room, and David stood watching the door shut behind him, once again surprised and more than a little confused at the lieutenant's actions.

He slumped into his seat, letting his thoughts flow freely. If he chose that option once he left the nest, he'd be his own master to some extent. He'd always be welcome back, according to Javed, Xavier, Celina, and to some degree Hope. Cressida had also reiterated that during their brief discussions. It wouldn't be cutting the cord completely.

The door opened again, and Genevieve wandered in. "I heard the boss was here. Was he looking for me?"

David indicated the seat, and she slid into it as if it were a daily occurrence. "Not exactly. He wanted to find out when you'd be back at work. The report I got today says tomorrow is fine, so long as it's light duties."

Genevieve rolled her eyes. "I asked them not to tell you. I was coming to discuss it."

He grunted. "That's how it works in nests, Gen."

She blinked at the shortened name. "I like that."

"That I knew before you?"

Her laugh soothed him as nothing else ever had. "No, dummy, Gen. I could learn to live with that. My friends, when I was younger, would call me Genny or Vieve. Maman just calls me bebe, but I like Gen. It's grown-up and just between us."

He glanced at her soft eyes and wondered if she realised just how much of the brash facade had worn away in the last couple days here with him.

"So?" she prompted. "He said...?" She cycled her hands, urging him to expand the conversation.

"He asked me to work for the Liaison Division."

Now she blinked, mouth falling open. "What?" She rose from the chair, stalked around to his seat. "What do you mean?"

He couldn't read whether it was apprehension or pleasure, just that she demanded an answer.

"There're problems with vamps. He's looking for someone in the know. Someone who knows things and people."

"You're going to accept it?"

"I don't know. I need time to think. I mean, I know I said I was going to consider it, and I will. But I also want to continue with my work on the vehicles." He shook his head, confused.

WHEN GENNY RETURNED TO THE PRECINCT THE NEXT DAY, SHE wasn't sure quite how she felt about the concept that she might end up working with David. On a daily basis.

They'd spent a lot of time together over the last few days. She learned he was funny. That he hated aubergine but adored sprouts. Particularly Brussels sprouts. He preferred his meat blue and was a neat freak.

She'd learned he knew everyone's name. Took pride in being able to solve a problem, but he had a secret love of cars and design.

He preferred the left-hand side of the bed. The truth was, she probably already knew more about him in a short period of time than she'd ever known about Julien in the years they'd been together. David instinctively knew when to hold her close and when to give her space, something Julien hadn't really cared about, if she was honest with herself.

She wondered what else he'd learned about her. Probably lots, given the way the house members talked about him being shrewd, quick, and sharp.

Could he also tell that she was terrified to the core that she'd fall for him and he'd find something about her, a failure he couldn't abide, and leave her on her own? The very thing her father had done? And Julien?

Walking into the precinct with him at her side was discomforting. What if they didn't last, and she had to work with him? Could she manage that?

They were waved into the boss's tiny office and took the seats he indicated. "You're improving, I hear. Light duties we can do for the next few days. Then we'll see how you're coping before you're back on the street. But right now, we've got a problem, and I need both of you. David, I've spoken with Master Javed, as I need you to consult on a new case. It's"—the boss shrugged—"it's an odd one."

Genny blinked. She'd never seen him quite at a loss like right now. "Boss?"

"I want you both in on this. We've got a vamp issue. It's strange. We know some vamps choose not to live in nests. They form enclaves, though it's not formalised. They owe no affiliation to the houses or the Council. Nothing new there, but in the last year, we've seen the enclaves grow. They're restless, and now they're spilling over onto the others. We've got shifters talking about bloodsuckers targeting their numbers for illegal gambling. The debts are enormous but being forgiven in exchange for grooming youngsters. Trafficking in sex workers and violent attacks."

Genny thought about her informant. "I wonder if this is somehow connected to the rogues we picked up at the mercantile."

The boss growled. "Could be. Might not be. But we need intel. David, you're—"

"He's a civilian, boss." It was hard to remain anchored to her seat, but the denial escaped. "I can—"

"Stop!" The single barked word silenced her.

David cocked his head. "I have a few contacts. I can chat with them, but it will take a few days. I'd need to find them, and these aren't questions that can simply be launched into."

Boss nodded. "Javed said he'll be busy preparing for some big event."

Judging from the way David's eyes narrowed, he knew exactly what Javed had talked of, not that she knew. "I'll have to split my time between the nest and here for now. I should have info in the next few days."

The boss nodded again. "Take a few days. We've got time, and I think there are pressing matters concerning Attar. Genevieve, you've also been granted the leave you requested for this weekend. Take it. Attend your brother's wedding, but be back Monday morning."

The dismissal implicit, they both rose. But before he shut the door, David turned back, and she heard his words. "I'm considering that offer."

THE FILES THE LIEUTENANT WAS ABLE TO SUPPLY WERE SCARCE, AND David flipped through them quickly.

"Our first step will be to meet and interview the informants on the list. We should also check out the enclaves. Get an idea of how many. You could then maybe ask some questions about who knows anything, if possible. See if you can get an idea of who these new vamps are. What they might be here for. Yes?" Gen's words were soft and measured.

He nodded, looking at the addresses. "Those are on the south side. All cheaper addresses and farthest away from most of the known vampire addresses." She glanced at him, and he shrugged. "They like to live at least within the same postcode. It's, I suppose, a hangover from the days when those loyal to nests needed to be within a reasonable location in case they were called upon to serve, and also for safety."

"Huh. I guess that makes sense, but did they really face—"

David nodded. "Yeah. Whole histories that we teach the younger nestlings deal with the mass attacks. In 1604, there was an attack on a London residence, which ended up with thirty-four dead. Only the master, his second, and the family of the *Yeux Secondes* survived."

When she gaped, he scratched his head. "That was the beginning of the House Regent in Gloucestershire. Before that, it was the House Belmont, but with the widespread losses, the initial house was dissolved and reconstituted. In 1905, just before World War I, the House Meyer was disbanded and all the members sent to America. They eventually became the first house in Los Angeles and assumed the name Mayor. It was the second largest house in the United States at that time."

"Wow. I guess I didn't expect you to have a history of houses like that. Or to be able to just... you know, roll it right out."

"Your clans don't?"

He noted the surprise on her face. "Well, I... Yes. I should have realised."

"We, nestlings and vampires, have many things we keep to ourselves, Gen. It's how we've survived for centuries hidden away from the greater human population."

"Of course. Your family, have they been nestlings for a long time?"

David smiled. "Our first nestling was a descendant of a distant cousin of Jean Ribault, a naval man. My family were Calvinists, but within three generations, they'd moved away from the belief system that had seen them hunted out of France. The story goes that the head of the household cast one of the granddaughters out, as she'd become pregnant out of wedlock. Laurelle was found by a man who took her in named Samuel. According to what's been handed down, she was in a pretty bad way when he found her. Anyway, Samuel eventually married her and raised the child as his own, along with another five he fathered. I'm descended from the first child. Jean eventually went on to become a senior member of a vampire household, just as his adoptive father was. And thus began our relationship with vampires that we know of. The thing is, now we know, courtesy of my sister, Hope's, blood, that we carried a genetic predisposition to the varied incarnations. It's what makes us susceptible to the change. We haven't previously, however, had a vampire within the family. This generation, there are three."

"Wow..." She stared at him. "That's going a long way back. And to know it all. We have some oral history, I guess, but I don't really know it."

"That's okay, you have plenty of time to learn it."

She laughed, but it was a harsh grating sound.

"I guess I do. Hundreds of years of it." Then she rolled her eyes at her own words.

The curl of heat in his belly rose, but any thoughts were swiftly dashed when the man called Julien entered the room. His gaze dropped first to Genevieve, then narrowed when he looked at David.

"What is he doing here?" His tone dripped with derision.

Genevieve raised her head. "The boss wants a consultant on the ground with knowledge of vampires—"

"We don't need no *zozo santi* here."

Her face turned red, eyes flashed with fire, and she rose. David reached for her hand, not quite sure what he'd been called but the curl of Julien's lip telling him it was derogatory.

"He just insulted you. I won't stand for that." She was already out of her chair, fists balled.

Julien's face turned bright red. "What? You're going to protect him? You sleeping with him now? I shoulda known better than some *mutt*—"

Now David surged up. "Do not ever use that tone with her. Never again." He got up close, gripping the man by the shirt and lifting him. Something deep within him, a fury, burned bright and uncontrollable.

The urge to plant his fist in that face rode him.

Others crowded round. Gen gripping his hand broke through the haze of red clouding his vision. "Don't. David, he's not worth it. Let him go."

Others were pulling Julien back with words of "What were you thinking?" and "What the fuck?"

David turned to her. "You were ready to hit him first."

She sighed. "Sure. But that's me, not you. He's a shifter, David, and you're human and liable to be killed." Her face softened. "I don't want that to happen."

A voice boomed through the air. "Who started this nonsense?"

The room froze, but David turned to see the boss in the doorway, his gaze assessing who was being held.

"Delacorte, my office. *Now,*" the lieutenant ordered.

The younger man stumbled as the others in the room released him. He shuffled forwards as if compelled to obey, and his eyes grew round and flicked from side to side.

"I'll talk to both of you later." The rush of power slid over David before retreating.

"Shit!" Genevieve blanched. "I... I don't want anything to happen to you. It's my fault."

He glanced at her. "No, it's Delacorte's fault, Gen. He must be prepared to wear it if he's going to dish it out. Now, tell me, where first?"

She named a location, and he snatched up his keys.

"What...?"

David grinned. "I'm driving."

CHAPTER 14

Genevieve shivered as they entered the outskirts of town. None of the houses were well kept but rather looked more like the tenements of old time. The roads were pitted and the facades of the old buildings dirty and in poor repair. Very few cars edged the sidewalks, and those that did were clunkers of indeterminate age.

"Nice neighbourhood," David murmured as he parked the vehicle.

"You should stay with the car," she told him.

He merely laughed and added, "Safe as houses. Got an alarm system."

No alarm system could possibly be good enough, she thought, climbing from the vehicle.

He rounded the car to stand beside her, scanning the numbers on the buildings. "This one." He pointed and led the way.

Pricks of awareness left the nape of her neck itching. People watching. Or was it vampires? Night had drawn in, and she shivered. Like humans, she wasn't immune to the sensation of fear and doom.

He climbed up the steps leading to the door. They, like the road, were in poor repair. He rapped on the door, and it opened quickly.

"A *Yeux Secondes* and shifter come to visit? Come in." The woman at the door looked young, but Genny was sure she was much older than she seemed, the cadence of her words odd, as was the inflection of her voice.

David bowed. "We bid you a good evening, lady of the house."

Genny stayed close to David, in case the woman before them posed some kind of danger. "We're here on official business. You made a complaint about missing humans and para?"

The woman gave a short nod. "Indeed. I've been here a long time, as have my neighbours. We had good help, assistants and servants, but now they're gone. New vamps moved in, and suddenly those who have been here to help us disappear."

David took the seat she offered, and Genny settled herself beside him, muscles tense. "So why did you come to us? Why not the Council?"

The woman laughed. "Dear, I'm seven hundred years old. If by now I prefer the Liaison Division over the Council, that says something, right? I know from bitter experience they won't act for us. We are not members of houses. We're simply scratching out our living by observing humans, working with them. Many of us are employed in jobs that allow us to continue being what we are. I, for instance, am an artist. I make jewellery of gold and diamonds. A skill learned long ago and refined."

"You're Orla Urretes?" David's eyes settled on the ring on her hand, then flicked up. "Beautiful work. Preference for diamonds, but any precious jewel on commission. I believe more than one royal family has pieces of your work in their collections."

"You do know your pieces, David. Your mother owned one of my chokers. I believe your sister, Mistress Hope, wears a piece custom-made for her. A ruby ring with diamonds?"

He gave a jerky nod, aware that Xavier, Hope's life partner and the master of the house, had commissioned it for her after they'd formalized their union.

Genevieve leaned forwards, needing to control the conversation. "So, you say they've disappeared. How do you know they didn't just leave? Return to family?"

The vampire turned, her smile condescending. "Many have lived with their families for long generations. My own servant, Anna, was with me since birth, as was her mother. Then one day, she went out to the markets and didn't return. All her things remain upstairs. She was twenty-four. For each year of her birth, it was my honour to protect her and her mother as they became my family."

"Could I see their rooms?"

The vampire grimaced. "If you must." She rose and beckoned them both forwards. "I know your reputation, David. I know the difficulties you've faced, as those among us who've lived outside have watched the nests rise in power. You're a good man. Find who did this."

If Genny were a lesser investigator, she'd take exception to the words. It was only that she knew the esteem David was held in that kept her response in check.

They moved up the steps, and the vampire, Orla Urretes, opened the door to a spacious living area, furnished simply yet with style and comfort in mind.

"This is where Carla lived with her mother, Elena. Elena passed away just over a year ago, but Carla didn't change anything. She said it was the home that was perfect and needed nothing done."

"Did she see anyone? Have a boyfriend or—"

"No. She was studying to be a psychiatrist. Had just finished the second year but was conscientious. Didn't want a boy because he'd get in the way of what she wanted to achieve. In the last few months, I'd been talking to her about moving. I wanted to sell, but she said this was home and if I would wait until she finished her degree, then perhaps we might relocate. She arranged for an agent to come through one evening about a month or so before her disappearance. Wanted to get some ideas about work that may be needed to increase the value."

David scratched his head. "You weren't present at the inspection?"

She shook her head. "No. We rarely attend those kinds of meetings in case something happens. I was instead next door, with my friend, until afterwards."

Genny wondered if the realtor might have some more information. Perhaps he might have seen someone or something strange. "Do you have a card or the name of the realtor?"

Orla squinted. "I think she put it on the fridge. It's what she did."

She flowed over and scanned the silver surface before plucking a piece of pasteboard from under a magnet. “This one.”

Genny looked down. The name wasn’t one she was familiar with. *More pieces of the puzzle, but no clear spot where it belonged yet,* she thought and pocketed the card. “Thanks for that. Here’s my card. If you think of anything that might be useful, let me know. If and when I have something to share, I’ll be in contact.”

She ushered David out the door, then looked back at the vampire standing on the steps by herself. There was a loneliness she recognised, and her chest ached.

DURING THE DAY, THEY VISITED ANOTHER THREE RESIDENCES. THE stories were similar. Families and singles with long association to a vampire. A “family member” disappearing, and not one of the missing over the age of thirty.

“This is odd, though. Why only young ones?” David asked.

“Do vampires prefer young blood?” Gen’s knowledge on the subject was limited—though she’d lived for a while in a nest, she’d been young and sheltered by not living in the main house.

“No, not really. Most vampires now live on the reconstituted blood. Many of these houses order from the distribution networks available to them. Very few feed directly from the vein, and those who do... they’re mainly the outcasts and rogues.” He shrugged as he steered the car through the gloom of night. “Those who live like Orla have been housed at some point in the past and chose to break away during times of upheaval in houses. Like when House Regent changed to Belmont and Meyer moved to Los Angeles.”

“There’s a point at which all of these must intersect,” she said.

As they drove through the large gates of the house, she sat up. “Why are we here? I intended on returning to work.”

He smiled. “Yes, but here I can spend time with you.”

She swung around to face him. “But you spent all of today with me.”

"That may be, but it was work time. This is us time. Different. If you want to go home tomorrow, I'll need to pack."

Shock coursed through her. "Pack?"

"Yes, I'll be coming with you. Though that will get in my way of running the nest." He spoke so casually she almost missed the meaning.

"Run the nest?"

"Yes. I need to meet with Javed and my staff. I have some things to sign off and some issues to address. It won't take long. You should shower and order a meal for us. Then I'll be with you."

"Wait." She felt railroaded, and she hated that. She balled her fists as her hackles rose. "You can't just decide where I'm going to stay, then decide that if I'm not here, you're coming with me."

"Listen, Gen. I have no idea what this is between us, but it means something to me. To you too, if I'm reading you right. But these are dangerous times. Being alone right now... We've got Attar and now this new vampire problem. Your old friend Julien is also pissed with us. So, yes, at this point in time, I can and will decide, because anything else just isn't acceptable."

No one, not even her *maman*, had ever put her safety and security first.

The confusingly mixed emotions were downright unfamiliar, and while a twinge told her it was unwelcome, the other side wanted to curl up and purr.

Shaking her head, Gen pushed that knowledge away. While it was lovely, it was more a case of would she be able to protect him? After all, he was only human. And he had his nest—

"I can read the thoughts in your pretty head, Gen." He leaned in and kissed her gently on the lips, and the taste of him pushed away all rational thought. "I will be sticking around."

He opened the car door, tossed the key to the young woman waiting, and stalked around the car to open her door before her rational thought re-established itself.

She shook her head once she was on the first step, grabbed his arm, and pushed him back.

Darkness flashed in his eyes, and he stilled her. “Don’t engage me unless you want to see what I can do.”

Genny blinked, but the words dared her inner creature to roar.

She moved quickly, lunging.

People came running, likely to save the *Yeux Secondes*, and she growled, “Stay back.”

He laughed. “I can handle myself.”

His eyes didn’t leave hers, and she wanted to scream at him, “Why are you doing this? I can really hurt you?” Controlling those words, she lunged, meaning to jab him in the ribs.

By the time she was in the position to make contact, he’d moved, dancing lightly on his feet.

Wait. What?

He assumed a position of a fighter, feet apart, fists up, and his face impassive.

This time she slid into a crouch and pushed hard, reaching for one of his legs. Again he’d moved, this time flipping backwards like a gymnast so when he came to rest, it was a distance away.

“So, you can move and deflect. What else can you do, pretty boy?” Her body loosened just a little.

He laughed, the sound full-bodied, while he assumed a relaxed pose. “Want to see, or shall I just list my accomplishments?”

It took long seconds for the words to sink in. Gen sighed and straightened up. “Accomplishments?” she parroted, genuine interest infusing the word.

“Ten years of gym, track while at school,” he listed. “Fencing, boxing, *rokudan* black belt in judo, and there are the official fighting techniques I chose as the son of the *Yeux Secondes*. I spar weekly with the vampires, am proficient with knives and the like.”

Her mouth surely must have been hanging open, because the list he’d just given had her head spinning.

Javed, the master of the house, ambled down the steps. “Officer Fernly, I believe?”

She gave him her attention, because he was downright imposing. The look on his face was welcoming, but she kept her wits about her in case he took exception to her attack on David. “Yes, sir.”

He reached for her hand and shook it. “It’s nice to see someone who can take on David hand-to-hand. He’s a bit of a dark horse, but he takes his training seriously. I wonder though, could I perhaps have a word with you later? In my office?”

She nodded, because how could she refuse a master when he wasn’t attacking her but instead requesting her presence?

“Then if I may, I need to talk with David. We have some business to attend to.”

“Sure... uh, yes, of course.”

David’s eyes glinted in the low light. “I’ll be up soon.” He touched the side of her face with a gentle stroke, and she leaned in, needing the touch more than she’d ever expected.

Then he was gone, and the people who’d come to his aid melted away so she stood there, feeling ridiculous and alone. Quietly, she entered the house and made her way up to his room. It was sparse, and yet in some ways it was honest in the scarcity of furnishings and adornment.

So different from her home, where she’d yearned for her own possessions around her. But this was him. What you saw was what he was. The urge to return to her home melted away as the realisation grew that this was the safest place for him at this time. He was human. Frail in a way she wasn’t.

Her cell rang, and she glanced down. *Maman! Rotten timing.* But then, there’d never be a good time to tell her mother about David.

“*Bonsoir,* Maman.”

“Bebe! I have heard strange stories about you from Julien’s family. What’s going on?”

Genny slumped down on the bed. “What have they told you?” She knew she sounded wary and weary, but right now, Julien’s machinations only made things worse.

“He’s been sent home after being attacked by a human. A human you’ve encouraged and... and *goaded* according to his maman.” The rapid breathing down the line told her Maman was reacting immediately from hearing the half-truths Julien had obviously peddled.

“Julien was out of line. He was angry that a house *Yeux Secondes* and friend of mine—”

"Friend? I heard he was panting after you like a beast in heat! What are you doing dallying with a human? You know better—"

"Maman! Enough. It's not like that. Julien is telling stories. Ones he's thought up because I won't go back to him."

"But he's such a catch, bebe. His papa is the beta of the clan. You'll be back among family."

"He attacked me, Maman. Called me a mutt!"

"Only in the heat of the moment, *ma petite*. I'm sure he didn't mean it..." Her mother's voice trailed away as if she was conferring with someone else.

Gen squinted and tried hard to separate the other voices muffled in the background, but she couldn't hear them clearly enough.

"Bebe, come home."

"I'll be there for the Joining, Maman, and David is coming with me. As my guest." She knew her mother wouldn't take that well, but what else could she do? She wanted him there. He had agreed to come with her in the last few days, and besides, being away from him... it left her feeling empty. He might be a human, but he knew their world. Was already a part of it.

"But, Bebe..."

Genny waited for her to continue. The discussions on Maman's side became muted, and Genny wondered again who her mother was talking to.

"Fine! Bring him, but don't expect more from me."

The sheer petulance in her mother's voice angered Genny. Hadn't she put up with a lot because of her mother's choices? Weren't they why she was an outcast among the clan? She inhaled, holding on to her anger. "You will make him welcome. He is a *Yeux Secondes* of a very important nest and my..." Shaking her head, she refused to say the words that rose to her lips, instead uttering, "He will be my guest. An honoured guest, Maman."

She hung up, but her hands shook with fury. "Why, Maman? Why do you do this?" She stalked from one end of the room to the other. She had almost blurted out that she wanted to take David as her mate. Except she wasn't really a shifter. *No, you're nothing. A hybrid abomination. Neither shifter nor human.*

Claws ripped through her fingers, the creature demanding release, and her shattered emotions couldn't hold it back. Instead, she cried out as bones cracked. "*Nooooo!*"

Words were impossible, but she closed her eyes, battling furiously. *Not here. Not now. Back! Sleep, cat. Time to sleep and rest. Soon. I will release you soon.*

Tears seeped out, and she panted, chest heaving with exertion until finally it subsided. Each breakthrough was growing stronger. The time between shorter. The hunger deeper.

The door opened, and David walked in to find her crouched upon the floor. He slammed the door shut and ran to her, his face drawn. "Gen?"

"The creature... I need to let it out soon." She heaved, glancing up at him, aware of the stink of sweat from anxiety and the sheer effort of soothing the creature that she exuded.

"Gen, there're places here..." He gripped her hands, as if that alone could soothe the raging fire inside. "We have a secure space if you need—"

But she shook her head. "No. Soon, but not yet. When we go down to my brother's Joining, I'll have to let it out then. You'll stay with me?" She bit her lip, because this exposed the deepest fear she had, that he'd turn his back on her because of what she was.

He joined her on the floor, enfolding her in his arms. "I'll stay with you, Gen. Whatever you need, I'll be."

She let herself sink into the reassurance of his embrace and inhaled the scent of him. His hands traced soft circles over her back as her breathing quieted.

While Genevieve slept, David held her close. He'd seen the way she struggled with herself. The emotional toll of whatever had caused her to leash the inner animal.

An hour or so later, he received a text from Javed.

<If Officer Fernly is available, would she be willing to meet with me?>

<Something happened after she came upstairs. She's exhausted and sleeping, Javed. Is there something specific?>

The three dots on the screen told him the vampire master was tapping away. It took a long time before the words flashed up on the screen.

<No. I'll talk to her another time. Sleep well, friend.>

He grunted. It wasn't that he and Javed weren't friends, but David took his responsibilities seriously. He'd been trained that it meant due deference, correct forms of address, and ensuring the master always felt he was the most important person in the nest.

Do as I say, but not as I do. The thought frittered across his mind.

His father hadn't stuck to the precepts he'd battered into David. No, he'd instead embezzled, lied, and sold his son to a woman with no care for the damage she wrought on her husband or his innocent sister.

"And I'm a fucking basket case."

In his arms, Genevieve muttered and turned, instinctively burrowing in.

David closed his eyes, more than aware that nothing could be fixed right now. It wasn't nearly enough, but he'd have to make do. For now.

CHAPTER 15

Like all good officers of the law, Genevieve understood that much of their work was hours of tedium, checking paper trails and looking for links. Normally she was more than comfortable with that, but today, it wasn't easy to accept.

David had remained at the house. He had work to do, and she'd been driven—*a personal driver assigned*—to ensure she'd arrived safely.

When the boss came traipsing out, she swore under her breath, more than a little aware that she'd prevaricated her way through the door.

"Progress?"

She turned her head so she could look up at him. "Not really, no." The words escaped with a frustrated tone. "I've looked for like crimes in the human population. None. The only crossover I can find is they work for vamps. They're not housed. There's not the violence we've seen with the Attar attacks, and they're all good people who pay their taxes, attend school or are self-employed." She scrubbed at her eyes.

"Hm." He picked up her notebook, read the page, then set it down. The pad looked tiny beside his meaty platter-sized hands. "Go home."

Genevieve blinked. "I beg your pardon?"

"Go home. Take a rest. You're away this weekend, so take it early.

When you return next week, your head will be clear and you'll think better. Go." The boss shooed her with a large sweeping motion. "Get out of here."

Genevieve was as committed to her job as anyone, but she didn't need to be told again as she rose, gathered her purse and keys, and headed for the door.

Even as she made to turn, the boss was snarling. "No. Nothing's going to happen, but if it does, we'll cover it."

Scurrying down the steps, she looked from her car to the stores on the opposite side of the road. Several boutiques, a salon, and a lingerie shop. She rarely had time to stop and think of things she really wanted. But not today.

She hurried across the street and into the shop with dresses and gowns filling the window. Slinky pieces. She wondered what David would think of them—or more accurately her in them. And even better, out of them.

"Can I help you?" A woman dressed in an expensive black-and-white dress with pearls at her throat sashayed forwards. Her hair was elegantly piled on top of her head, her make-up a shade too close to perfection for Genevieve.

"I'm looking for a dress. Or a couple. Something not over the top. Not formal, but you know." Genny waved a hand at her body. "For me. I need..." God, this was so much harder than she expected. Normally she dressed in pants or jeans and tops. But with David, she wanted something... hot!

"For an event?" The woman's perfectly arched eyebrow rose as she walked around Genny. "I have one or two pieces that might suffice."

Genevieve wandered behind the woman, who beckoned her to a corner of the shop, and watched the careful arrowing, hand flipping through hangers.

"This one. I think this one too, and maybe this?" With three dresses in a grassy green, a turquoise, and a scorching red, she was pushed into the dressing rooms. "There's one other, and I'll grab it too. It's a very chic noir piece from an up-and-coming designer."

The curtain shut behind her with a determined swish, and Genevieve took a moment to put down her things and stare in the mirror. The one she saw, she knew well. Her figure trim, with firm high breasts and a waist that flared delicately. The array of dresses hung in her periphery. She'd need shoes, something knockout, but the colours of the dresses were each startling. Without thinking, she slipped the red one off the hanger with one hand. The texture was soft and the material lightweight, and she scrambled out of her uniform and had it unzipped in record time.

The fit was glove-like as it flowed over her body, touching where it was supposed to, and the colour was a foil for her hair. "Yes." She rehung it and popped it on the other hook. The second was the turquoise. A silk mix if she didn't miss her guess. Once again it was an exquisite fit, with delicate cutwork around the neck and hem and finished with tiny cap sleeves. "Also a yes."

The green one was a thing of mastery. A halter-necked sheath with a lacy insert at the bust. "Must have this," she muttered as the woman clucked on the other side of the curtain.

"I have the other one."

Genny slid her hand out to take the gown.

The lines were classic, three quarters in length. Tiny straps moved over the shoulder, and it went on with a sigh, the fabric a luxurious dupioni silk that shimmered under the lights. Everywhere it touched was magically enhanced, she thought.

Without checking the prices on the tags, she slid it to the pile of haves and dressed quickly.

Refusing to consider that this shopping blowout might not be the perfect solution to her problems, she exited the dressing room. "I want them. I'll also need accessories. Shoes and bag," she clarified, and the woman smiled.

"Of course. This way."

Within minutes she'd bought a pair each of nude, black, and red court shoes—her mother's term for pumps—with spiky heels and matching bags. With her wallet considerably lighter, she exited the store. She hurried back to the car and slid the bags onto the back seat.

Her expedition only just started, she headed back across the road to the salon. It was quiet, and she smiled. "I need my hair cut."

One of the three stylists glanced up and down at her. "What are you looking for?"

Genevieve grinned and explained, then moved to the back of the work area with the woman. An hour later, her hair was just above her collarbone, the natural curl bouncing freely.

She had one last stop before heading home, and she intended to make it worthwhile.

DAVID LOOKED UP AS HIS CELL PHONE BEEPED. "DAVID SPEAKING."

"What are your plans for tonight?" Gen's voice was thin and high. Excited. He couldn't contain his pleasure.

"None so far. But do you have something in mind?"

"Dinner at my place? I'll order something, and we can finalise my packing. Maybe an early bedtime before we leave in the morning?"

He laughed out loud. "Maybe a few of those, but not everything. I've got my bag packed, and I've organised a driver." A glance at his watch filled him with pleasure just as the sound of the shutters rolling down echoed. "I'll be on my way in about half an hour."

She disconnected, and he closed the folder he'd been working through. He and Javed had spent time over the last few days preparing the house for its third *Yeux Secondes* in its short life. The relief he'd experienced in completing his task of shortlisting the final candidates was difficult to describe. He felt sadness to be leaving this place, and yet it was also the right choice.

He'd been born and raised to know he had a place and a role, but his entire life had been of someone else's choosing.

He was free to make his own decisions and mistakes. He'd effectively remain a member of the household but make his own choice as to employment. While the suggestion made to him by the lieutenant was certainly of interest, there was still only one choice of career that drew him.

His work on the cars was important. It would make a difference to those who needed the ability to travel safely, and he'd managed to secure an agreement from Javed that they'd back the fledgling company as minority owners.

Now, with the agreement in place, his personal life could become his prime concern.

Genevieve.

This weekend would be hard on her. He'd already made discreet enquiries as to who was likely to be there. Including Julien Delacorte, the pampered second son of the beta of the clan. He wondered how Gen hadn't even known him beforehand.

His mother's favorite, from what he could ascertain.

Genevieve's ex-lover and the man who'd called her a *mutt*. His blood raced at the memory of the pain on her face. "I won't let him hurt her again." But how could he protect her if they weren't in a formal union?

He rose and moved to the door, waiting for the sound of Javed's footsteps. He'd taken to rising early, as both Javed and Celina were involved with preparations for the battle against Attar. A cruel and ancient vampire who posed a significant threat against them all.

The door opened, and Javed moved inside. "Ready, then?"

One glance at the master vampire's face and he felt guilt. "Tonight?"

Javed shook his head. "No. Not tonight, but soon. We've got information and are training now. I'm hopeful, with the right tip-off, we'll find his lair and be able to defeat him. But that's for the massed vampire faction to attend to. You'll be fine?"

Their friendship had taken time to grow. David joined the nest at a time when upheaval in his own life had made him terse and unfriendly. "Yes. We'll be back once the immediate ceremony is done. Gen doesn't wish to stay because her mother is difficult."

Javed opened his mouth.

"Gen's words, not mine. She's also worried that Julien Delacorte will be there and cause problems."

Javed clasped his shoulder. "You'll do fine, I have no doubt, but if you need assistance, the local nest has offered support."

The words took David aback. "You've spoken with them?"

Javed gave him an abashed smile. "You're family, David. It's what they do."

He could only nod his thanks.

"Now, are you on your way?"

"Yeah. Look, if you need me—"

"The house has been trained to care for itself. You've hand-picked and trained your assistants. They'll manage for a weekend. Besides, if something does happen, you'll be back in time to pick up the pieces."

It didn't sit well, but time was passing, and he wanted to be on the way to join Genevieve, so he nodded, scooped up his bag and the laptop satchel he was taking, and headed for the door.

"David?"

He turned. "Yes?"

"I like her. Bring her home with you." Javed's eyes glinted in the evening light with humour, and David simply shook his head as he left.

BITING HER LIP, GENEVIEVE CONSIDERED THE TABLE. THE WHITE cloth, candlelight, and the places she'd set. Her apartment was small—compact, she remembered from the advertisement—but the perfect size for a single. Having David here reminded her that it was also very intimate. That had her fanning herself for a moment, remembering the many and varied ways they'd now christened just about every useful surface in the place in the last few weeks.

The meal sat in the kitchen on warming pads, and she waited anxiously for David to arrive.

What would he think of her dress? She'd chosen the red one for tonight and taken care with her hair. Anxiety unlike anything she'd ever experienced zinged through her. She stalked to the small stereo and turned the dial, seeking something soulful.

It felt like hours had passed before he finally knocked with an imperious rap at the door. She'd been in the force too long to take it at face value and checked through the peephole. Warmth flooded her body as she spied him there on the landing, and she opened the door, ushered him in.

His bags dropped with a thump on the floor as David's arms wound around her midsection, tugging her close.

The heat of him surrounded her, invaded her skin, and his scent rose. Dark and musky and oh so male!

"I like your hair," he whispered, then leaned in to kiss her. Heated, it scorched all the way down to her toes. Lips moved, mobile and firm over hers, dragging an arch of her spine and a groan from her. He lifted his head. "You look good enough to eat."

"Eat? Oh! Dinner!" She tugged from his hold, wishing she could stay there in that safe harbour, but the food was going to cool if she waited too long. "Sit down. I've got wine and food ready."

She bustled to the kitchen, wishing she'd delayed the delivery by another hour. But if they had, it would have been more likely Chinese or something similar they could share naked on the lounge, under a blanket. Tonight she wanted to show him how much his support meant to her.

Instead she fussed, serving the red meat with the hearty red wine sauce and the steamed vegetables. She carried them out and set them on the table before returning to the kitchen to pour two glasses of the red wine as accompaniment.

He'd settled at the table, and his eyebrows arched. "Celebrating something?"

"My leave, your being here. Time alone. Take your pick."

He laughed. "Well, any of those will do as an entrée, then."

They ate, chatting about their day. When the meal was done, he thoughtfully gathered up the plates and carried them to the kitchen, and she leaned against the benchtop, watching him fill the dishwasher and dispose of the remains.

"I finalised my tasks with Javed today."

His words slowly filtered into her brain.

"To step down?"

He nodded. "I made my decision too. I wanted you to be the first to know. While I'm happy to be a consultant to the Liaison Division, it's the car design that I'm going to continue with."

Twin emotions rippled through her. Dismay that they wouldn't be together but joy that he'd decided his future.

But that meant he'd be homeless. Something unfurled inside her chest—hope. "What about where you'll live?"

It wasn't something they'd discussed, but perhaps...

"Well, I'll still be part of the nest. I guess I could request an apartment, but I've already seen somewhere. It's just a matter of whether there's room." His face tightened, cheeks turning a ruddy colour. "I don't suppose you've room for a housemate, do you?"

The unfurling emotion bloomed, and she couldn't control the grin. "I think, so long as you don't have too much furniture, I could find space."

He licked his lips. "Well, actually... I know this is your place, but I was thinking more along the lines of we find somewhere together. A little bigger, with an extra room or two. For down the track. I'll need an office." The shrug he offered reeked of concern, and she considered his words.

"I'm not sure how quickly I could sell this place."

David shook his head. "You can keep it if you like, as an investment. I've got more than enough equity to buy something outright."

"I..." How was she supposed to reply to that?

"Or we could buy a house, with a yard. Something just out of town, if you want somewhere to..."

The words died away, but she knew what he was thinking. The sweetness of the offer nearly overwhelmed her, but she battled with the emotion. "That's honestly the nicest thing anyone has ever offered me. Maybe we could talk about it tomorrow. Right now, I'm feeling stuff that's..." She waved a hand in the air, used a finger to swipe away the moisture pooling at her eyes. "Come to bed with me." She reached out and tugged him to the short hall to the bedroom.

Instead of simply complying, he scooped her up in his arms and strode in a determined and manly way to the bed before lowering her to the floor beside it. "I don't want to ruin your dress. It looks lovely on."

Devilry filled her as she considered what she wore beneath it. The lacy blue bodysuit she'd purchased just today.

"Unzip me," she invited and turned her back to him.

His hands fumbled, and she restrained the giggle that wanted to bubble free. The dress gaped finally, and she slid her hands free so the material dropped in a pool at her feet. Now she turned, and the hissed exhalation told her the choice had been correct.

"That should come with a warning," he muttered as the green of his eyes darkened to pools of desire.

"Perhaps," she answered and slowly leaned down to gather up the dress. "But it seems you're now very much overdressed for the occasion."

Strains of soulful music filled the air as she watched him, hands moving as he released the buttons of his white shirt. But much as she loved him in a severely tailored black suit, Genny was more than pleased he'd shucked the jacket during dinner, along with his tie.

As he shrugged free from the shirt, Genny watched beneath half-lowered eyelids and licked her suddenly dry lips. "My, what an impressive physique," she murmured, reaching forwards to slide her hand along the exposed skin of one pectoral muscle.

Before he could move towards her, she danced away, aware of the way her body moved in the outrageous covering she wore.

He groaned and closed his eyes, but not before the desire in them settled on the mounds of her breasts with hunger.

"Remove some more, lover boy, before I get any closer."

His hands wrenched at the belt, and her body heated, noting the tenting of his pants. The rip of the zipper filled the air, and she couldn't contain the sigh of pleasure as he also shucked his underwear.

"Fuck," he muttered.

"What?"

"I didn't take off my shoes."

Genny giggled at the absurdity. "Then let me assist." She lowered to her knees at his feet.

His cock bobbed before her, and she eyed it with hunger. Slid her tongue between eager lips and swiped over the engorged head.

He hissed. "Gen..."

"Just returning the favour," she growled before returning her attention to the task. Gen quickly unlaced the black leather at his feet, and he grunted at her. "Lift your foot."

Finally divested, he swooped down and lifted her.

"You're a dangerous woman, Genevieve Fernly." His mouth covered hers with an intensity that seared her. His tongue surged within her mouth, and she relinquished her hold on reality, letting herself fall into the maelstrom of eroticism he'd introduced her to.

A hand toyed with the strap of the bodysuit, wormed its way beneath to trace the lines of her collarbone.

He ripped his mouth away, and they both gasped for air. "You're so damn sexy, and this should be a concealed weapon, but how the hell do I get it off you?"

His demand was dark and filled with intensity.

"The crotch. There's..." He turned her, kissing the side of her neck, and she arched, desperate to give him better access while nerve endings snapped and hummed with desire.

"Gen?"

Unable to see while lost in the throes of pleasure, all she could do was mutter brokenly, "Oh... God! Snaps."

His hand covered her breast, tweaking the nipple through the lace and silk before soothing the sudden sting with a soft swipe of his thumb.

The hand slid down over her belly, and it tensed in reaction. She sucked in an unsteady breath as it slid lower, between her legs.

"Fuck, you're so wet already, Gen."

She could smell the scent of her own musk on the air along with his. Entwined and heady.

"Fuck me, David," she demanded.

"No, but I'll love you."

In her heart, the rhythm set up a wild dance.

Their mouths met, and, and she felt him fumbling between her legs for the snaps, felt them give. Once again, he traced the edge of her jaw while his hands tugged at the bodysuit, stripping her. He only disengaged to remove the garment, then with care pushed her to the bed, following her down as the mattress dipped and swayed.

Pleasure speared her as his fingers combed through the downy hairs at the juncture of her thighs, finding the treasure hidden between the folds of skin.

"Wet and hot," he murmured while the slide of skin-against-skin pushed her hunger. Inside her belly, something twined deeper, an invisible coil of emptiness that could only be filled by him.

"David, please," she entreated.

"Soon."

She writhed, fingers digging into the bedding, clutching tight as he drove her deeper into the ecstasy-filled space only they inhabited. His mouth settled on one peak, his lips around the tip, and she bucked as a flash of pleasure streaked through her breast to groin.

"So responsive."

Heels dug deep into the coverlet as legs widened to grant him greater access and his mouth continued the torture as it slid over exposed skin of her belly, tongue dipping into the hollow of her navel.

"Please," she moaned, her fingers twining in his hair.

"Soon," he answered once more, and she bucked when his breath whispered over her core. Lips settled on her, and she cried out as the sudden climax ripped through her. "David!"

The scream couldn't be contained as her grasp of reality shattered.

When she was able to regain some control of her mind, it was to feel him crawling back up her body, his face filled with hunger.

"I love you, Gen." His gaze bored into her, as if demanding she understood the importance of his declaration.

Her eyes watered. "I love you too, David." Now as he moved, she made herself watch his face while he positioned himself at her centre, cock ready to begin the hot wet slide that joined them.

"I want you, Gen. I will always want you."

Her hands settled on his shoulders, gripping tight.

"Please," she panted, the heat flaring inside her once again.

"Now," he murmured.

This time her body took control, legs sliding around his hips, pushing him deeper.

Inside the cat stretched, demanded, and with a surge she had no hope of controlling, her teeth descended and she sank them into his shoulder as he moved.

"David!"

He bucked and danced. "I love you," he chanted, his mouth now settling against her, breaking the skin. Not that she felt the burn, too lost in the wild joining.

The rhythm was wild, cataclysmic, and their orgasms flashed hot.

The roar of a cat inside her mind, warning her even as she rode the storm.

Finally done, she collapsed onto the bed and he on top of her.

Gen caught sight of the dribble of blood.

Dread formed in her belly. "Oh... fuck!"

His hand cupped her cheek. "What?"

Her eyes met his. "Did you bite me?"

David frowned. "What?" Confusion darkened his brow. "What's wrong?"

Genny swiped her hand across her mouth, noting the scarlet liquid, then held her hand up.

His eyes widened, moved side to side. "Genny?"

"Did. You. Bite. Me?" She spoke deliberately as fear welled, its greasy waves replacing the repletion.

"I... I think so. Yes."

Her eyes closed as reality slammed down on her. *What the fuck have I done?*

"Gen?"

"Have you been checked? I mean your blood?" This time when she opened her eyes, she took in the concern on his features.

He nodded.

"I could have..." She gulped. "What if my bite makes you sick, David?" Questions crowded her mind. *You're a fucking mutt. It's probably not possible.* Surely her hybrid status should keep him safe? She just didn't know. The lore said it took two in order to complete the circle. To make them truly one in blood and bone and to change a human. But not being whole herself... Maybe she didn't carry enough of the strain to change him. If it had, they had time before they'd know, if she remembered correctly.

His hand covered her shaking one. "If I am, then so be it."

The depths of his acceptance humbled and scared her.

To David's pleasure, it seemed Genevieve had packed before his arrival. Her single small suitcase sat beside an overlarge handbag near the door. He hadn't noted them on his arrival, and this morning, as they'd woken entwined in each other's arms, he mentioned she'd need to hurry.

Her laugh filled the air. "Already done, David."

Now they reclined in the seats on a plane. He'd insisted he should make the booking, and she'd been horrified initially when their tickets revealed he'd booked Business Class. "But I can't afford this!"

He'd cupped her cheek. "No, I redeemed loyalty credits. It's okay."

Emotion swam in her eyes. "But I don't like—"

"I know. I should have asked, but the option was there, and I wanted us to be comfortable."

She'd finally acquiesced, and he was pleased, given the pounding in his brain and the heat that chased along his nerve endings.

When the attendant brought water in a glass, he'd gratefully accepted it, drinking it down as thirst raged.

"Are you okay?"

Genevieve's quiet question broke into the strange fugue that settled over him. It sounded like she was talking through some kind of veil, blunting the clarity of her voice.

"Yeah." There was no way he planned to share just how "off" he felt.

Her eyes betrayed her concern even as she nodded. "Okay, but if you need something, tell me."

"Sure," he muttered and hunkered farther down in the seat. Perhaps if he slept, he might recover enough to get through the weekend?

That was a false hope, as once the plane touched down, his entire body ached, the pain in his head threatened to erupt through his skull, and his eyes felt swollen and gritty.

Genevieve touched a soft hand to his forehead. "This is rotten timing for a flu."

"Yeah," he grouched. At least his stomach wasn't uncertain. That, however, was a small mercy.

Genevieve organised a hire car, and he waited as his body assumed what was nearly a meltdown. His temperature skyrocketed so that by the time they were settled in the vehicle, every inch was scorching hot.

"You need a doctor," she said, concern threading her voice. "Antibiotics."

"No. It's just the flu. I'll be fine." What else could it possibly be? He'd been inoculated for every virus possible, and he'd not been near anyone who could potentially be ill. "Unless...?"

She shook her head. "It's usually days before symptoms emerge, as I recall. Not like this at all."

He couldn't concentrate on direction as she drove down long winding roads and into the surrounding countryside with towering trees. He became aware of a hum, not that of the car engine but something else. Maybe it was the movement of the blood in his veins, he thought, then nearly laughed out loud at the ridiculousness.

The glances Gen kept giving him were redolent with fear. "When we get to the house, I'm going to call the doctor. You're sick."

David didn't bother to argue, because he felt worse still. Clearly he'd picked something up and didn't want to share it on. He'd have to hide out during the Joining at this rate, and it appalled and frustrated him that the one time Gen needed his support, he'd be unable to lend it.

The trees were lusher now, the sky hidden from view, and he felt his lids growing heavier. Sleep was calling, but he fought it off. "Tell me about your family."

"Bastien is my twin. We're fraternal. Bastien is fully Were. I'm not, as you know. We thought my father was Luca Thorne, until it turned out he wasn't." She sighed and looked out the window. "She was wild in the early days of their marriage, and one night, she went hunting for something better. That resulted in me. Luca wasn't, shall we say, happy when he realised I wasn't sired by him and cast my mother out. Bastien and I were young, so we went with her. Not that Bastien was keen on that. He returned to the family as soon as he was able, joining Syrah and Franc. They're both older than me. A lot older. Syrah is forty-three and still young by pride standards. Franc is sixty next month."

He frowned, realising he hadn't known she had other siblings. "Are they also joined?"

"Syrah joined with Caleb Thornton nine years ago. Franc's wife, Emma, passed away about eight years ago. She gave birth to my one niece, Eliza, who lives with him within the clan house. She's ten."

"You use the terms clan and pride. Why?"

"We're cats. Big cats. We've got a few mountain lions and panthers. When we use the term clan, we mean the greater body. The pride is our family unit."

"Ah."

"David?"

He turned his head, though now she was a fuzzy outline against the darkening sky. "What?"

"They aren't very welcoming. I mean, they'll probably be hostile towards you and me." She spoke so quietly he had to strain to hear the words.

"Why?"

"Because of who I am. What I am and what I'm not. Then I'm bringing a human in, and they don't care about your association with the houses, because all humans are lesser beings in their eyes. Unwelcome. By bringing you as my guest, it's one more infraction against their beliefs."

He heard the fear and worry and reached out.

"I'm sorry I've caused you distress." He really meant it, but there was no way he'd have wanted her to come by herself anyway. Not after the way she'd been treated by her so-called family.

She pressed the indicator and took a smooth turn onto a well-maintained track. The green canopy melted away under the rolling of the wheels until finally they entered a glade.

Buildings dotted the landscape, redwood log houses, the largest set towards the back of the long driveway. No fences, he noted, just grass waving in the breeze.

She pulled the car to a stop at the large house. "We're here."

CHAPTER 16

David wavered on his feet, and Genny slid her shoulder under his armpit, holding him upright. He was heavy, and she sweated as she assisted him up the steps, more than a little aware of the burn of gazes drilling into her back from the houses nearby.

The creature rose up, close to the surface, and for the first time in many years, she let it stay, aware an attack might occur at any second.

The door slid open and Maman stood there, her auburn hair waving around her shoulders, her golden eyes piercing, and the look on her face tight with distaste for the man Genny was half carrying.

"Will you help me get him inside? He's sick," she muttered. Her mother simply opened the door farther and stepped aside. Fury boiled in her gut at her mother's insult, but she whispered to David, "Come on. Let's get you into a seat, and then I'll call the doctor."

Not much had changed, and for now she was grateful as he sank down to the lounge just beside the door. The bags would wait; right now her first concern was to seek care for him.

"Is the doctor still on call?"

"You're more worried about *him* than kissing your maman?" The hiss was low, and Genny's hackles rose.

"Right now? Yes."

Another door opened wide, and Luca Thorne entered the room. “What are you doing here?”

Her gut might have started churning, but she’d learned a thing or three in the police. “I’m here because I was recalled for the Joining. As Bastien’s twin, it is both my right and my duty.”

“I’ll have no *mutt* in my house.”

Once, the taunt would have burned her. This time she stood her ground. “I don’t plan to stay here. I will, of course, take one of the outlying guest houses, but my… friend is ill. He needs the doctor.”

Luca sniffed, the wide flaring nostrils moving as he tasted the scent of the man who’d travelled with her. “He’s not human. What is he?”

Genny barely stopped herself from grinding her teeth together. “He is. He is also a *Yeux Secondes*, so he should receive every courtesy.”

Luca whirled, his black eyes gleaming. “Don’t threaten me, child. You will regret it.”

“No threat,” she replied. “A promise. The local nest knows he’s here and why. They also know about me. About this clan.”

Luca advanced, and it took every ounce of willpower to remain exactly where she was, between Luca Thorne, her mother’s husband, and David, where he lay supine now, having slumped farther down.

Her mother advanced, crouched down. “What have you done, bebe?”

Every muscle tensed as she watched her mother expose his shoulder. The bruising round the bite zone red. She cursed. “Fuck!”

“You bit him?” Her mother’s eyes bored into Genny’s, and for the first time, the panic threatened to overwhelm her.

“I…” What on earth? How was she supposed to answer that? “Oh yes, Maman. We had hot sex last night, and I lost myself. Bit him in the throes of my orgasm”?

Her fingers rose, covered her lips as her mother pinned her with a glare. “Stupid girl! It looks infected.” She sniffed and frowned. “It doesn’t smell like it, though.”

Luca shoved her aside, and her hands balled into fists. “You bit him?”

“Yes.”

“During sex?” he queried.

"I..."

He snarled and turned. "Was it during sex? Yes or no?" The words were hard, and something primitive rose inside her.

"Yes!" She bellowed her answer because all she wanted to do right now was gather him up and get out of there. Not an option, though.

"Did he bite you?"

The question blindsided her. "That's none of your business—"

"Bullshit! Did he bite you? It's simple. Yes or no, Genevieve?"

She shook, fearing she'd somehow caused this illness that manifested. "Yes, okay? Yes! I bit him, and he bit me during sex last night. Is that what you need to know?" Tears threatened, and she dashed them away.

Luca growled, his hand flying through the air towards her. A meaty fist connected with her cheek, and she snarled, her inner predator erupting uncontrolled.

Body cracking and fur sprouting.

Except she wasn't fully cat. Her nails became claws and hair sprouted, teeth elongating and her body lengthening. Her exposed skin took on an otherworldly golden hue. The cat woman stood before them, inserting herself between the man she loved and the people she'd protect him from.

Luca laughed now, the sound caustic.

"Step away from him." The sound was a growl of warning, but Luca ignored it, crouched down, and touched the wound on David's shoulder.

"Well, we'll have to see what genetics she has. What he is once the change is complete." He rose and retreated, crossing his arms over his wide chest. "Vivienne will call the doctor. Once your friend is able, you'll move to house four. You will not go out except for the ceremony, and when it's done, you leave."

Genevieve's mother bit her lip. "I need time with bebe, Luca."

"At house four. Not here, Vivienne. I will not tolerate this pair of —" He appeared to struggle for a word before sneering. "—*them* in my home."

Her mother nodded and sighed. "Yes, Luca. Bastien will need to spend time with her."

Luca shook his head. "No. He has other things to focus on. Gina must not be tainted." God, how those words pierced Genny. Reinforcing that she didn't have a family. "Your behaviour put our entire lifestyle at risk, Vivienne. Syrah and Franc have wisely chosen to stay at the other end of the village and won't be mingling with them either."

Vivienne might have dropped her head at Luca's words, but not before Genny caught sight of the rebellious light in her mother's eyes.

David grunted, and she whirled, the creature once more subsiding as she knelt beside him. "David? Can you hear me?"

His eyes opened, though they were glassy. She turned and noted Vivienne had a cell phone in her hands, talking to someone.

Her mother turned away and soon replaced the phone in her pocket. "Doctor Henri will be here soon. But if Luca's theory and mine is correct, by tonight he should be feeling better."

Genny screwed up her nose. "What? You think you know the cause?"

Her mother sighed. "So much I should have explained. Once we're in house four, I'll tell you what I can."

"Vivienne..." Luca's voice interrupted, warning his wife.

Vivienne whirled, her face tight, body stiff.

"This is *my* daughter, Luca. You washed your hands of her years ago. Told me you wanted nothing to do with her and she was my responsibility. You will not now tell me what I can and can't tell *my* daughter. You got what you wanted that day." Her voice rose with fury. "Any right you had to direct our relationship died when you cast us out."

Luca's eyes widened, and then his legs moved him up close and personal with Vivienne. "I am the head of the clan."

"To hell with that, Luca Thorne!"

It was the same old same old for Genny, though. The relationship turbulent, though never violent. Their rages well known, along with the making up. More than once she'd woken in the middle of the night to the sound of their lovemaking. Weres were dramatic and easy to rouse, both to anger and intimacy.

"I..." David's slurred voice reminded her he needed her assistance, and she focussed on him once more.

"Shh. It's okay. The doctor is on his way. We'll work it out—"

A knock on the door had her spinning. Henri, the grizzled medic, entered.

"Someone needing my assistance?" His gaze settled on Genevieve with shock and surprise, then David. In a split second he moved in, displacing her.

Vivienne stepped up, hovering over Genevieve's shoulder. "She bit him. During sex. And he bit her."

The man swivelled. "What? So, he's..."

Her mother managed a gallic shrug. "So it would appear."

Henri grunted and turned back to David. "List your symptoms."

David rattled off, "Headache, wooziness, exhaustion, muscular pain, temperature," while Henri checked the bite point.

The man scratched his head and rose, turning to Genny. "Show me your bite point."

She blanched, feeling cold fingers of dread sliding into her stomach. Nonetheless, she pulled aside the light top so he could palpate the area with a grunt. "It's too soon," she muttered.

"You haven't educated her?" He aimed the words at Vivienne.

"I haven't had a chance."

"You've had years, Vivienne. The girl can't become what she truly is, if she doesn't know about her heritage—"

A snarl emanated from Luca. "She's not—"

Henri shook his head. "She is. Whether you want to acknowledge it or not, she's enough were to have infected him. She may also be other, but putting your head in the sand and refusing her knowledge endangers her. As a result, you endanger us with your blind devotion to purity. Your mother warned you before her death. You know the words as well as I do."

Genny's gaze narrowed at the bellow from Luca of "Get out!"

Henri shrugged and retreated.

"What words? What don't I know?"

Luca pinned her mother with a glare. "You cannot tell her. I forbid it, Vivienne."

David felt better by degrees as the day wore on.

They'd moved to what Gen called house four, explaining it was the least salubrious of the guest housing, on the very edge of the village. He didn't care. The bed was soft and cosy, the bathroom efficient but fitted with a hot shower which he'd already used satisfactorily. The kitchen, miniscule though it was, was stocked with meat, vegetables, and fruit along with coffee.

There wasn't a sitting room, as the place was essentially just a large single room with a burner in the corner for winter. David remained where Gen had laid him down, watching her mother, Vivienne, stalk around the room. She almost forgot he was there, and that suited him down to the ground.

"There is a prophecy, you understand, given generations ago, that one would be born. A child of strength who would cross the boundaries between were and others. One who'd be the balance of future prides."

"But what does that have to do with me?" Gen's voice rose, and he waited as Vivienne paced.

"Bastien is better with his knowledge of the lore. Luca has been teaching him. He'll be here soon and can explain it."

"No, *Maman*, you tell me," Genevieve entreated, but her mother simply shook her head.

It sat on the edge of David's tongue to remonstrate with Vivienne that as Genevieve's mother, surely she shouldn't abdicate things of such importance, but he wisely kept his mouth shut. After all, it wasn't like his own family were better at keeping things together. His parents hadn't bothered to make contact since leaving the house they'd ruled for decades.

A rapping echoed, and Vivienne rushed to the door. A large man, his hair the same colour as Gen's, entered the room. He appeared not much older than a teenager, yet he knew instantly this with Bastien, Gen's twin.

"You came."

"Maman said you wanted me here." The cold between the two almost turned the inside of the house frigid, and he understood for the first time just how Hope must have felt. His gut lurched at the pain on Gen's face.

"Yeah." Bastien looked down. "It's not that I don't appreciate you making the journey, but Gina doesn't know about..." He waved his hands.

"That I'm a *mutt*?"

Bastien growled. "Don't say that." His eyes shone in the deepening gloom.

David moved in the bed, and Bastien's eyes widened. "Papa told me about him. You bit him."

Gen's face blushed beet red. "Does everyone?"

"Just about." Bastien shrugged. "Has he changed yet?"

Gen's nose wrinkled, and David cleared his throat. "I showered. Do I smell?"

Bastien laughed. "Neither of you knows? Maman?"

"Luca forbade me to tell. He didn't forbid you, though." Vivienne wrung her hands together.

Bastien sighed. "It's got nothing to do with smelling... David, is it?" He took up a position in an armchair. "There's a prophecy. One that was made centuries ago. It says that one day a child will be born. One who is not pure. That this child will breach the distance between were and others of the world. That this will be because, in a moment of true love, they'll change the one who will walk beside them during the term of their unnaturally long life."

David blinked, not really expecting this at all. "That's..."

"One hell of a prophecy. The clans are big on keeping bloodlines pure because they like being separate. They don't want to mix with others. That means that anyone birthing a child who isn't pure is turned away. Except in our case, because Maman was only away one night, and her girlfriends didn't realise she'd hooked up. My... her husband didn't know Genevieve wasn't his. It was only at puberty, before her first change, that we worked it out."

"I'm so sorry, bebe. It was never my intention to make such a mistake." David saw Gen flinch, though he doubted her mother noticed. "I didn't know I could get pregnant twice in the same heat cycle. I'd been with Luca and thought I was safe. Luca and I… it was never a love match, and we agreed, so long as I was careful, that any other interactions would be forgiven. Until you." Vivienne covered her face with her hands.

During the speech, Gen had blanched. "Mistake?"

He doubted her mother heard.

Bastien's face tightened. "You're not a mistake, Gen."

She turned, her eyes glittering. "*Maman* just said it. I'm the mistake the clan would rather do without. Gina isn't supposed to be tainted, and Syrah and Franc want nothing to do with me." Every sentence was a knife, and Bastien winced.

"It's not that simple, bebe," Vivienne whined.

Having had enough, Daniel dragged himself from the bed. "She's a strong woman, but you have all done your bit to destroy her. Not one of you stood up for her when she most needed you. She's lived with verbal barbs all her life and made herself into a woman I am proud of."

Bastien's gaze settled on him. "David. You are a *Yeux Secondes* of an important nest, I understand. You walk with feet in two worlds, yes? But now you should prepare to enter a third. If the prophecy is right, when you were bitten, you were infected by the were virus."

David blinked. "Were virus?"

"Consider the prophecy. Think of what I've said."

Gen dropped to the seat. "But I'm not a full were."

Reality impinged on him. "This isn't a sickness?"

"No sickness. You're changing. Becoming a were."

SILENCE FINALLY DESCENDED AS MAMAN AND BASTIEN DEPARTED, leaving Genevieve and David alone in the tiny cottage. Her stomach grumbled, and she wondered about making some supper. Nerves quivered because she'd done something that could only be considered unconscionable. She'd taken his choice from him.

Hands settled on her shoulders. "Gen?"

She stared out the window, fear stabbing deep. "I didn't know, David."

"I understand that, Gen. I won't regret what we have either. If this is indeed what it is, we accept it."

She whirled. "But how can you—"

"Shhh." His hands gripped hers, the pressure grounding her. "One of these days, you should ask Hope and Celina about their changes. Neither had a choice. Daniel, my cousin? He's the only one who chose when he became life partner with Cressida, the head of the Council."

Frustration ate at her. "But you should have had a choice. This is no different to my mother and her lovers. I mean, she's not a particularly good wife, as you've heard. Their marriage was arranged, and she was wild..." Gen shrugged because she really didn't know how to explain properly the regret she felt. Not from being with him but taking away his options.

"It'll be okay. We'll find a way and muddle through. Now let's get dinner done. I'm starved. Then perhaps we can go to bed. And cuddle if you prefer."

Such earnestness filled his features, and she leaned in, welcoming the heat of his hug. The embrace soothed the creature within.

"What if your creature is as misshapen as mine?" The words tumbled out against his chest.

"We'll deal with it when the time comes. Because I love you, Gen."

Her heart stuttered. "What? I thought it was the heat of the moment or..."

David's fingers bit deep, and she pushed him back so she could look into his eyes. "Listen carefully. I'm a man who's made mistakes. I don't have a lot to offer right now. The security of my position isn't going to be there much longer. I'm making a new and honest life, but the one thing I've learned is that love is the foundation stone I want to build my life on. Yes, this is quick, and I know you're unsure. But I love you, Genevieve Fernly. You're the woman who saw the man I hid from others. You're the one who healed me. I'm not asking for any great declaration."

Her eyes leaked tears as she listened to his words. God knew she wanted to believe them. "I..." She licked her lips and his gaze followed the action. The deep green of his eyes heating with sensual hunger.

In response, her body tightened, and suddenly her mouth was covered by his, her fingers spearing deep into the dark silk of his hair.

His hands found her hips and tugged her closer so the hardness of his erection poked at her belly.

Carnal hunger roared inside her.

"Fuck me, David."

He laughed against her mouth. "Never. But I'll love you. Hard and fast or soft and slow. Whatever way I can get you. Because I'm starved for you and you only, Genevieve."

She arched, his mouth gliding along the line of her jaw before slipping over the thudding vein of her neck. His hands trailed down her back, caressing and curving over the line of her ass, and she shivered. Then he tugged her closer so his cock slid against the centre of her while she twined her legs around his waist.

"I'm going to push inside you, so your hot wet pussy sucks at me. You're going to cry out my name when you come all over me. Then I'll ride you some more."

His words, dirty yet arousing, had her breath hitching. "Yes... I want you like that. Here, on the bench... now."

Hands pushed at her, repositioning her butt, and she found herself seated at the very edge of the wooden bench. His hands dove beneath the light cotton of her skirt, sliding over the skin of her inner thighs, and she squirmed, aware that she was so turned on, she'd drenched her panties.

"Yum. Wet, aren't you?" His fingertips toyed over the silk covering her mons. "I'm not going to rip them, but they're coming off, Gen. Then I'm going to put my mouth over you. My fingers will play, slide over your clit and deep inside you, and make you hotter."

She gulped.

"Is that what you want?" His demand was coupled with a finger sliding over the sensitive core of her.

Oh God, did she ever! "Yes," she breathed as her eyes fluttered closed, their weight too much in her frenzied state.

He hooked a hand under the band as she sucked in a breath, her body a wild buzz of nerve endings.

"What do you want, Gen? Shall I love you like that, or do you want me to suck at you? Lick and drink until you scream my name?"

His voice filtered over her, a wave of primal desire urging her to demand anything he had to give, so long as the orgasm her body craved lay at the end of their play.

"I want you. Inside me. Filling me up." The words were broken as she tugged at her shirt.

"No. Leave your top on for now or I'll get lost in your luscious breasts. They're so beautiful, with hard tips I want to suck. But if I do that, I might not get back to your pussy, and it's craving the attention right now, isn't it? It wants my mouth."

"Yes," she answered, body tensed as his words wound her hunger tighter than before.

His hands moved, sliding beneath the silk and pulling them away. Baring her to his gaze. The whisper of his breath, and she jerked back with a soft moan. "Ready for me?"

"Oh... please." His mouth descended on her, touching her and drawing her deeper into the web of pleasure.

She writhed and arched while he devoured. Every glance ricocheted through her body until she exploded on a cry.

David hefted her up as her body clenched in the afterglow of the orgasm. His mouth against hers, tangy. Musky.

They moved; she didn't care where because the thrust of him against her over-sensitized skin wound the invisible wire within her once again to a level of excitement. They tipped onto the bed, and he rolled her over before reaching for his pants. Shucked them in record time and crawled up and over her.

"I want you, Gen. However I can get you. You're like a fever in my blood, and I don't want to get better because you feel so damn good."

Their gazes met, a silent union taking place as he lined himself up, his cock at her entry. "When I'm inside you, I feel like I'm home. Complete." The slide was slow, measured, filling her body. His words though, they filled her heart.

Tears pricked at the backs of her eyes.

His brow creased, and he stilled, embedded deep. "What's wrong?"

Gen raised her hand, caressing his cheek. "Your words are beautiful, and I want to be worthy of you."

"You already are."

The first rock had her gasping, the second bowing off the bed as they came faster and wilder.

"I love you, Gen. You have to know that."

"I love you too."

He rode her mercilessly, and she loved it. Taking every move and slide and wanting more while her heart crashed and thudded, her body beaded with sweat that mingled with his.

He reached out, and she took his hands just as the climax loomed.

She shattered. A million tiny star tracks stealing her sight.

David tensed, giving over to his own pleasure with a grunt of satisfaction.

When he slumped down, it was into her arms, where they lay intertwined, regaining their breath, his hand moving in lazy circles over her skin.

"I didn't think you were a dirty-mouthed kind of guy."

He stilled. "You don't like it?"

She smiled. "I like it. A lot, in case you missed my reaction."

He laughed. "Just checking. Anything for my lady."

"Is that what I am?" she wondered aloud.

"Today and every day. Now sleep. There's lots going on tomorrow."

CHAPTER 17

David watched as Genevieve left him at the bar, his drink warming. She'd been quiet through the ceremony. How much of that was because of Luca Thorne and his attitude, or Julien shooting daggers at them both? It might have been the man who was the clone of Thorne, with the child sitting beside him during the Joining, or the woman who appeared to be a mini-me of Vivienne.

"She's coping well." An older man of grizzled appearance dropped into the seat beside him.

"I beg your pardon?"

"Genevieve. She's had a tough life. Luca's threats against her were the reason Vivienne fled, taking those two with her. The child was banished because of something she didn't do. Then when she returned, Luca made it clear she didn't belong. Julien blindsided her. She came back here, looking for a place among the police, and he... he dazzled her, strung her along because it was in his best interests. He knew who she was, whose daughter, and he used her until he realised Luca wasn't going to change his mind."

David turned. "Do I know you?"

The man grinned. "You clearly don't remember me from yesterday. I'm Henri, the local doctor and, of course, a shifter. I was the one who delivered Genevieve. Patched her up after she broke her arm and was there after Julien's attack."

David's gut lurched. "The scar on her chest."

The man nodded. "She's a good girl. Been treated badly, but I've been watching you. You're caring for her. So, I'm going to give you a tip. When this is done, get her out of here. Don't bring her back. If Bastien's guess is right, and mine, she's in danger until she can sort out what else she is and learn to accept the power. Tell her to find the prophecy and learn it. There's more to it than what's commonly spoken of."

The man pushed away from the bar.

"How do we—"

"Tonight, friend. You need to leave tonight." Then he pushed his way through the throngs just as Genevieve returned.

GENNY'S EYES DARTED AROUND THE ROOM AS SHE SLID BESIDE David. The reception building wasn't large, but there were nooks, mostly near the bathroom. Nooks where she didn't want to get cornered again. Her skin crawled, remembering the brief run-in she'd just had with Julien.

She exited the bathroom, ready to find out if David had seen enough. She'd shown herself, made the mandated "appearance," but she knew she was little more than an outsider. No one came close to chat or share a drink. She and David had taken up a position near the wine bar and even served themselves.

The door closed behind her.

"Ma coeur." *Hands slid around her midriff, and she jumped.*

"What? Fuck, Julien, I've already told you it's done between us, so get your filthy paws off me."

He growled in his throat. "Come, my love. You adore me, and that pretty boy human is only a foil..."

His words slurred, and she rolled her eyes. "Get lost, Julien. I've got no interest in you or the ridiculous plans you seem to imagine I'm going to fall in with."

Julien lurched closer, and the stink of liquor rolled off him in waves. She wrinkled her nose at the stench.

"You need me. No one here will accept you. If you were with me, things would be better. For both of us."

Now Genevieve frowned. "What? I don't want you, Julien." She pushed against his grip, and he released her with a sneer.

"Too good for me, are you? Well, you're wrong. I'm willing to take you on out of pity."

The words might have sliced through her before, but not now.

"The only pity partnership I foresee in your future is the fuck you'll get if some stupid dog takes you on," she hissed and strode away.

In her mind though, she wondered what he thought he'd gain by waylaying her and making out that he wanted to be with her. Then, with a shrug, she pushed the thought away.

She slid her hand into his as they stood together by the long wood bar. "What did Henri have to say?"

"He suggested we should leave. Tonight."

Her gaze narrowed. "I think he's right. Let's blow the joint. Bastien knows how to contact me, and I hope this time he'll try to stay in touch. If not..." She shrugged, but he could read the hurt and disappointment.

"Your mother?"

"I'll ring her later. We should head back and load up the car."

They returned to the house, hand in hand. Within an hour, they were driving out the road, and David watched the tension seep from Genevieve. "The ceremony. It's more formal than I expected."

"Oh. Well, I guess it is, but you haven't seen it all. Tomorrow is the full moon. Traditionally the family chooses that time for the Joining, and the happy couple will shift and hunt together. It's the final part of the ritual, if you will."

"You don't need to stay?"

"I wouldn't be welcome."

He frowned, remembering the distance between her and the others. "You wouldn't want to come back here sometime down the track?"

Her head turned. "No. I like where I live, and I really enjoy my job —most of the time, anyway."

"And Julien?"

"He's a pain in my ass. I can only hope that he won't return to the Liaison Division. Working with him daily is going to be hell." Her eyes narrowed. "Especially after..." She shook her head, and he placed a hand on her thigh.

"After what?"

"He tried to corner me by the bathroom. It's odd, though. He broke up with me, then turns up far away from home. Claims he's missed me." She shrugged. "I'm just reading too much into it."

The thought that Gen was telling herself that she read the situation wrong sat uncomfortably, though. In his experience of time with Genevieve, she not only trusted her instincts, but they also were rarely wrong. David filed the information she'd shared away for now. Perhaps later something about it would make sense.

"It's going to be too late to fly out tonight." She smiled at him. "We could maybe get a room. Somewhere quiet and soundproofed."

He laughed. "Ahh, I've turned you into a sex goddess, then, or at least a nymph who likes dirty talk."

She giggled, and it warmed him all the way through to his bones. "I don't know that I'd go quite that far, *mon coeur*."

David's pulse rate spiked. "What do you have in mind?"

"I know of this little private hotel. Very comfortable. On the way to the airport, but out of town. They do a mean meal as well."

He nodded. "Drive on, then."

CHAPTER 18

They reached the gate at the airport just as her phone blared. "Fernly here."

"How soon will you be back? There's been a development in the Attar situation. We need you and Mr Jardin at the precinct." His voice was firm, but she heard the hint of excitement there.

She glanced up, the flight board spinning. "We're about to board. We can head straight there from the airport, boss. But I won't have my gun or—"

"Doesn't matter. We need you two specifically."

"All right," she answered, but the call had already disconnected. Nerves below the surface started to jitter, and David quirked a brow at her. "The boss. Something is going down with the Attar situation, and our skills are needed. We need to go directly to the precinct." Questions lurked in his gaze. "I don't know any more than that, so don't ask."

They took their seats, and though the journey was swift, it was still several hours before they touched down. Time enough to wonder what on earth might be going on.

"I'll get the bags. You meet me out front with the car," he urged, and she took off, turning on her cell as she did, checking for messages.

But there was silence. By the time she'd made her way to the pickup area, he was waiting, and she sprang out, assisted with stashing the bags in the trunk. The car hummed as it traversed the roads, while every moment her brain told her to hurry.

They drove into the precinct in the late afternoon and entered the building.

The boss called them back as soon as they entered, and with her hand firmly grasped in David's, they followed the hulking man to the rear.

Once inside the conference room, he sat them down beside a young woman, her face bloodied, and a blanket wrapped around her.

"Emily here was found near a warehouse. She was brought to us because the regulars didn't know what else to do with her. That was last night. However..." He turned to the girl. "Emily, do you mind?"

The girl flinched as he gently bared her neck for their view.

"Shit!" David shot from his chair. "Attar?"

The girl's eyes widened farther, not that Genny would have thought that possible, and the last tinge of colour in her face bled away.

"Don't... please, don't hurt me," she whispered.

Genevieve moved forwards, taking her hand and holding the girl's gaze.

"We won't. You can trust us. We're the good guys, and we are going to find who did this." Her mind spun, trying to make sense of what she was seeing. The Council would need to know, and aware that the hunt for Attar was their priority, she knew she'd have to take the girl to Cressida. An old and very powerful vampire. One she hadn't met but who was life partnered to David's cousin, Daniel.

Her gaze caught with the boss's. "I need to take her to the nest. They'll need information, and while we can probably ask questions, they know what facts we might miss, to fill in the gaps."

The boss nodded. "Yes. But you two should take her. You've got the relationship with them that none of us have."

She bit her lip because there were now even more complications. How would they take that? David had told her about their run-ins with the matron and shied away from the idea that perhaps his situation might be compromised by what they'd done. Even if it had been an accident.

"David?" She whirled towards him.

"I'll come with you, but you're the lead. Cressida will know what's needed." He didn't reach for her, but it was as if his words caressed her cheek and offered her support.

She rose and left the room, seeking her desk. Ringing any of the nests was a trial, but to ring Cressida herself?

With shaking fingers, Genny dialled the house and asked to speak with Cressida. Not that the receptionist was very willing. She had to explain who she was, then wait while they checked her credentials, she guessed.

Eventually she was put through.

"Cressida." The voice was carefully modulated with a tiny hint of an accent. French, if she didn't miss her guess.

"Councillor? I was... uh, it was suggested that we should contact you." Stupid to feel so off balance, she told herself, but this woman was immensely powerful and had the ability to make David's life hard if she put a step wrong. David had told her she was lovely and welcoming, but... well, it wasn't that she didn't believe him, but he'd grown up with her.

"And you are?"

Genny blinked and wondered why that information hadn't been passed along. "Oh, apologies... I've never spoken to a vampire mistress before. I mean, a Councillor..."

"Well, now you have. How may I help you?"

Genny hissed her frustrations at herself, then realised the woman would have heard that and winced. "I'm Officer Fernly with the NYPD Liaison Division, and we currently have a woman here claiming she was attacked by a vampire. Except he doesn't sound like any kind of vampire we've ever heard of. We were wondering if... I mean, given the circumstances..."

A long second passed. "Indeed, you need us to talk to her. To try and find out who and where?"

Genny hoped the woman would say yes. "Yes. We think she may be another one of Attar's survivors. We can bring her to you, as we know about the situation with the creature we're hunting."

"Of course, Officer. When should we expect you?"

So simple, but an immense hurdle she'd overcome in one quick call. But nothing was certain with vamps, and she'd be taking David with her. "It'll maybe take us an hour or so, but that means—"

"We can shelter her here until tomorrow, or if she fears our kind, I can arrange for her to be transported to one of the other residential facilities while we rest along with our human staff."

"That would... Uh, if you could."

"Perfect. We will be awaiting your arrival."

Returning to the room, she crouched before Emily and quickly explained what had been arranged. Then they bundled the girl up and got her settled in the car, but not before Genny realised they needed to distract her. "David here grew up in a nest. He knows the vampire we're going to see."

Emily's eyes shot to David, who nodded. "Sure did. Grew up in the same house for a long while. She won't hurt you. All they want to know is what happened and where. But we'll stay."

"We just got back from a break down in Georgia. Ever been there?" Genny asked.

"No."

Monosyllabic answers weren't exactly conversation, but it was a beginning, so she started talking about the trees. The Everglades and the meal they'd eaten at the tiny restaurant. Emily did relax a little, at least easing the white-knuckled grip on the rear door, and Genny didn't have the impression the girl would rather fling open the door and throw herself into the traffic than meet with the vampires. *It's a good thing she doesn't know about shifters and weres, then.*

They turned into the driveway, and she slowed. "I'll stay with you, Emily, if that's what you want?"

"I... I'm scared," she whispered, and Genny could feel the anxiety on the air.

"I know, but they won't hurt you." She stopped the car at the steps, and the three of them climbed from it. She took Emily's hand, and David moved before them as the doors were opened for their entry.

"David!" a voice called, and he turned. Daniel, David's cousin, waved him forwards.

They conferred for a moment, and then David turned. "I need—"

On his face she read his concern, but she shook her head. "It's okay. Emily and I can do this together."

They entered a room full of vampire masters. She recognized Xavier, and Javed nodded at her in welcome as they settled. Soon after, Daniel joined them. It took a great deal of willpower not to ask where David was. If he could have joined them, he would have.

Emily's hand twisted in Genny's as if she were afraid to let go but scared of everyone in the room. Genny couldn't blame the poor girl. She'd had no experience of vampires until now, and suddenly she was thrust into a nest after another had attacked her. "It's okay."

"Do I have to do this?"

Genny patted her on the hand. "I'll stay, Emily. I promised, didn't I?"

"But they're vamps... like he was."

Xavier half rose, then shifted his glance to Cressida and settled back in his seat. Genny wondered if Mistress Cressida had sent him a mental message, then discarded the thought. It wasn't important right now.

Emily rose as if ready to bolt.

"Emily? Will you come and sit down? We'd like to ask you some questions about the vampire who attacked you." Cressida patted the chair beside her

Emily started and looked at Cressida with horror. "What do you...? They know. They probably want to—"

"No, Emily. Officer Fern...?" Cressida looked at Genny as if asking for assistance.

"Fernly, Councillor. Genny Fernly."

"Officer Fernly explained that you'd been accosted by a vampire. Emily, we're searching for one. I need to ask you some questions. To work out if it's our quarry. If it is, then you'll be helping us to..."

Emily twisted her hands and settled back down beside Genny.

On a sigh, Daniel reached out and touched the girl's hand. "He's been killing humans and vampires alike, Emily. You trust the police, don't you?"

"Good. Think of us like the police for vampires. It's our role to bring him to justice. Hold him accountable for the crimes he's committed. But to do that, we need your help."

"W-What do you need me to do?" She still sounded hesitant, and Genny was pleased that Emily's death grip on her hand released enough for the blood to begin flowing again, even if it did sting a little.

"Good girl. It's important that we know what he looked like and where he is."

"I can... I can do that."

They talked for a while, and finally Emily was comfortable to be settled for the evening in the human wing.

"Thank you for bringing her to us," Cressida said. "I understand you and David—"

The door swung open, and David stepped inside. "Sorry about that. There was a problem at the nest. They needed me to take a call and give some information." Now he bowed to Cressida, and the membranes in Genny's mouth dried, her body once more alive with his proximity.

"David, it's good to see you. Will you come and sit? We'll need to go prepare in a moment. We think we finally have the whereabouts of Attar thanks to Emily."

David shook his head. "No. We really need to get moving. I have things to attend to back at the nest, but..."

When he looked at Genny, she felt something else. The burning need that raged in his eyes. The one that never seemed to abate. She rose. "With your permission?"

Cressida rose and took her hands. "Of course, Genny. But do not let David become a stranger. He's been on his own far too long."

David blushed, and she felt the burn of knowing gazes as they retreated.

CHAPTER 19

David cursed his bad luck on arrival back at the nest. The vampires were massing for war, meaning important tasks he'd expected completed during his absence had not been.

"I need to go attend to a few things," he muttered as they entered the building.

She waved him forwards with a "That's fine. I know my way." He watched for a moment as she started up the stairs towards what he now thought of as *their* room.

Inside his office sat piles of files. Some he'd work through today, but others would need to wait. It was the package that lay on the tabletop next to his computer that caught his attention.

A tiny card was attached.

David, it seems you've joined our ranks from what I've been told by the lieutenant. Welcome to the clan, and bring that delicious Genevieve with you. I've been trying to get her to join us for many a year!

Simon Bellingham

He blinked. Simon Bellingham used the official title Lord of the Lycans rarely, from what he understood. An Englishman, he'd emigrated during the early 1800s with his clan to the north of America, and while there were many non-affiliated clans—and he was willing to bet Gen's was one of them—he commanded respect from his peers and the vampires alike.

The packet contained a pair of steaks, and David laughed before pressing the key on the phone and asking someone to come collect it. "Maybe you could cook it and have it delivered to my rooms in about half an hour or so?"

"Of course, David. We'll arrange a meal. Would you like anything else?"

Genevieve. Naked. On my bed, waiting and willing. The thought was hot enough that his body reacted instinctively.

"David?"

"Uh... champagne and strawberries."

A long silence followed by "Of course." The line disconnected, and he shoved the note into his pocket. No need for anyone else to know until he was good and ready to announce his change of circumstances. Not that he really felt any different.

"We'll have to talk about that," he murmured and set to work.

***

The tray table was wheeled into the room just as David appeared. "I'm going to change first, and then we can eat."

He disappeared into the bathroom, and Genny wondered what he was up to. There was a bottle draped with a white cloth and glasses. Champagne flutes, she noted. The silver domes catching the light and a bowl of strawberries off to the side, a mounded dish of whipped cream, and the crockery and cutlery gleamed.

"Thanks," she muttered and latched the door behind the retreating back.

With swift moves, Genny set about preparing the room, glad she'd taken a moment to shower and dress in fresh yoga pants and a light top. *At least I don't look a hag.*

When the bathroom door opened, Genny was sitting on the bed. David emerged, a towel slung around his neck but dressed in jeans and a button-down shirt. His feet were bare, and for a reason she couldn't explain, that had her belly filling with heat. He made a beeline for her, and as he kissed her—a slow and infinitely carnal kiss—he snagged a strawberry.

"Hey!"

His grin lit up his eyes, and he settled beside her, whipping off one and then the other of the covers.

"Oh. Steak?" She turned to him.

"Ever met Simon Bellingham?"

She nodded. "Sure. A long time ago. He wanted me to join the pack, but I wasn't ready to make decisions. He's a good guy, though. Hasn't pushed me since."

David reached into his pocket and withdrew a card, passed it to her. She read the words, surprise filling her. "How does he know that?" She shook her head. "I bet it was Henri. He's got more connections than an octopus has suckers." The words sounded waspish even to her ears, and she slumped. "That was mean. Henri's a good guy."

David embraced her. "I can understand your frustration. Thankfully he doesn't seem to be needing an answer right now. But I've got a question for you."

The sudden nerves in his words had her turning, brow wrinkling. "What?"

"Marry me?"

Her jaw dropped open. Inside her, the curl of heat grew, blinding her because the emotions it carried were huge. "I..."

He cupped her cheek, swiping away an errant tear with his thumb. "I know it's quick, and I'm ham-handed, but I want to be with you. To share my life, whatever it is. Because you..." His voice thickened. "You complete me, Gen. Without you, I'm only half the man I can be."

"Yes," she breathed. "I will."

His lips claimed hers, and she let him gather her close. "After Attar, we'll share our news. All of it. Then we can talk about the future, that house we need to buy, and clans. But until then"—he pulled away—"we should eat."

CHAPTER 20

David set about following the precepts of war as set down by the manuals of the *Yeux Secondes.* For centuries it had been their way, and while he could swap carriage for car and runners for cell phones, the art of preparation really hadn't changed all that much.

The staff from the kitchen trooped into his office.

"We have the blooded wine prepared. Goblets? Make sure there's enough to go around several times over. When they return, they will require immediate sustenance. Also check our supplies of bloods for those injured."

A chorus of "Yes" answered, and he ticked it off from the list on his desk.

He turned to the armourers the house employed. "Weapons?"

"David, each vampire's individual weapon has been checked. Knives and blades have been sharpened and the scabbards laid out. Those who prefer UV weapons have turned them in for servicing and are laid out down in the caverns, as you requested. We've also added some whips and bats for those who've requested them."

Another woman raised her hands. "I've a supply of body bags prepared for returning any lost, and the vans have their shelves in place should they be required as funeral transportation. We've also managed to get the old ambulances prepared with emergency supplies of plasma until we can get them back to their houses for attention."

Burying their head in the sand and being ill-prepared for losses was neither strategic nor realistic, but hearing the work his people had done buoyed him.

"Cars and trucks backed up to the witches' cavern to receive the supplies," offered another of the nestlings, and David could just imagine the humans racing back and forth, hoping to ready what may be needed.

He cleared his throat, aware that silence had descended. "I've spoken with the lieutenant from the Liaison Division. Captain Usain has issued a warning to general policing staff and those in the Division to stay away." Voices murmured. "I will leave here and join my family this evening once the alert comes in. The house will lock down. No one in or out until I give the clearance order."

"But, David, what about our families?"

He eyed those assembled, aware that one false step now could undo all the work he'd put in preparing them for such a crisis.

"Bring them in. Have them here no later than one hour before nightfall. Once night settles, there will be nowhere to hide. Are there any further questions?"

Heads shook, and he dismissed them, his hand itching to reach for his cell phone to hear Gen's voice, but she'd be busy. They were setting barricades in place and making patrols, though they'd back off well before sundown.

It beeped, and he looked down, smiling as he noted the message from her.

<Will be home soon. We've been relieved of our tasks.>

David huffed out a breath, relieved to know she'd be with him when the time came.

He rose and headed to the office. He'd move upstairs and dress. Cressida's house didn't have many humans, and he along with others hand-picked would be ensuring the safety of the Council residence during the attack. Genevieve at his side.

The black leather pants were reinforced with a light but durable substance. Not quite bullet- and knife-proof, but it would give them some protection. He tugged off the button-down shirt and replaced it with a T-shirt, then donned his leather jacket. He wore boots, light enough to not impede but with reinforced metal toes and a nifty switchblade in the front.

He ordered a meal to be shared in the dining room with Gen once she'd dressed in the jeans and jacket she'd laid out just before heading into the precinct this morning. His nerves jumped and quivered until he saw her enter the room.

They didn't talk as she stripped off and headed for the bathroom. There wasn't much left to say for the moment, but they let the kiss and touch of hand on cheek communicate for them.

Before leaving the room, he watched as she slid around her neck a pendant of gold adorned with the coin her mother had sent.

"Ready?"

She took his hand. "Yes."

Together they descended the stairs, a united front. Celina and Javed had stayed during the day at Cressida's, along with Hope and Xavier, so he and Gen would offer the solace and support to the house.

They settled at a table in the centre of the room, having agreed to eat early before they were due to head to Cressida's house. Those who joined them in the dining room were sober. Very few spoke, and those who did kept their voices low. On the nestlings' face, he read concern but a readiness to offer whatever service might be required of them.

His phone rang, and all eyes settled on him. He took Gen's hand. "David Jardin," he greeted.

"It's time. We have the location and are massing." Daniel sounded tired.

David looked to the front of the house. The shutters hadn't yet dropped.

"Understood." He dropped his fork and nodded to Genevieve, who rose.

They turned, hands gripped tight. "We must leave you all now. The Council house is unprepared. You are well trained, but make no mistake, the hour of danger is upon us. Take care of each other. Remember, a house can be replaced, but those who make it a home cannot." He bowed deeply.

In turn, the nestlings rose and returned the action before he and Gen left the room.

"We'll win this, won't we?" the girl who usually parked his car asked as she handed him the keys.

He wouldn't lie. "I don't know for sure, Sarah. I hope we do. We're trained, but nothing is certain in life and death."

He and Genny climbed into the car, but as he drove away, he glanced in the mirror to see the pale-faced girl still standing there, watching him leave.

GENEVIEVE COULDN'T IGNORE THE BUTTERFLIES WHIRLING INSIDE her belly. Fear wasn't something she ignored but rather used to make her stronger.

Tonight, she'd need every ounce of strength she could muster.

She'd seen the twin of her fear inside David's gaze. The way he'd looked at his people, his eyes touching each one. Memorizing them.

Arriving at Cressida's nest, they climbed the steps together, hand in hand. The humans gathered didn't speak, simply took up positions at various points of the house, she and David at the main entrance. But they didn't speak either.

What more was there to say?

At midnight, they dragged chairs side by side and settled in them, just in front of the doors.

Every hour a slow trail of time.

By three, exhaustion pulled at her. Draining.

When the peal of a cell phone ringing broke the silence, she jerked upright. "Who?"

David dragged the phone from his pocket and glanced at the screen. "Javed?"

She didn't hear the conversation from the other side. Could only watch as the worry on his face lightened. "Fine. We'll see you soon." Now he turned and smiled. "It's done. Attar is defeated."

She almost deflated until he rose and tugged her from the seat, pulling her close. “Marry me, tomorrow night, Gen. You and me? What we have is special. Let’s formalize it.”

Heaven knew, the words he spoke warmed her in a way no others could. But was she ready for tomorrow? “I need a little more time, David. We need to do this right.”

His brow furrowed. “The dress? The soiree?”

She giggled at the dismay in his tone. “No. Not necessarily, but we’re talking about forever, David. Let’s make it special. Our combined family of choice.” She slid her hand over his cheek. “I know with Alexa, you had the whole nine yards and a lot more besides. I don’t want a society wedding, but I do want those who are most important to us there. I’d like to ask Bastien and Gina. I think he’d be amenable to bringing her over and I’d... I’d like to get to know her. Damn the taint.”

“Sure,” he answered, but she detected a note of concern.

“I’m not planning on changing my mind,” she whispered and kissed him gently. “Now, we should move these chairs back, out of the way. I don’t want Cressida on my tail because I rearranged her furniture.”

The house was once more settled by the time Cressida and Daniel, Hope and Xavier, along with Javed and Celina arrived. They didn’t linger long though, heading to their respective rooms, but not before Cressida announced that David and Genny should remain in the house during the day. Then they headed for their beds.

“They defeated Attar,” Genny murmured, watching them head up the stairs.

“Together they’re a pretty strong army.”

She glanced at David. “Yes.” Even as she settled in, her cell phone squawked.

“Fernly.”

“Bebe?”

She rocked upright at the voice.

“Maman?” Her mother sounded panicked.

“Bebe, I’m in town and must see you. It’s urgent.”

“I... Sure. Where and when?” Her mother might have been vacuous and more interested in her own needs, but Genevieve couldn’t ever say she’d heard this tone before. “I’ll bring David with me.”

"Why?" The genuine puzzlement overlaid the concern, and Genny almost laughed out loud but contained it.

"Because what affects me affects him too. We're together, Maman. We're planning to marry."

"No Joining Ceremony?"

Annoyance flashed through Genny at the sound of her voice, memories of Syrah's ceremony coming to the fore. The arguments and her mother demanding involvement as the "Mother of the Mate."

"If we do, it'll be on our terms, Maman."

"Fine," her mother sniped and then named a location. "I'm heading there now, so you should arrive in about ten minutes."

Genny bit her lip and glanced to David. "Thirty at least. I'm not in town." Without thinking, she disconnected and turned to him. "We need to meet with Maman. Let's go."

David's eyebrow raised. "Now?"

The sound of shutters broke through the near silence, and Genny nodded. "Yes, now."

CHAPTER 21

David rubbed his brow, trying to stay awake. They'd been on the go since early the previous morning, and he had to admit the fact that Gen still had enough energy to meet this latest crisis was admirable. If a little scary.

At the twenty-four-hour restaurant, she parked, and they climbed from the car. His gaze swept the nearly empty carpark. All he could see were a handful of cars and a motorcycle. A gleaming gold Debussy Eliminar. Beautiful to ride, worth a mint, the collector bike was a dream for most enthusiasts.

His glance settled on it, wondering who would be in a place like this riding something like that.

"It's beautiful," Gen said and swiped a finger over the seat.

He'd noted before her affinity with gold. Her jewellery was all old gold pieces. Memories surged, the way she touched the coin she wore as if it were a talisman.

They entered the building, and the first thing he noticed was Vivienne, sitting straight-backed in a chair, beside her a man with red hair and piercing golden eyes.

Genny's eyes.

Genevieve glanced from her mother to the man and back again. “Who is this?” she demanded.

Vivienne opened her mouth, closed it. Opened it again, and for a moment, David had the impression of a fish out of water, gasping for air.

The man rose. “So, this is my daughter, Vivienne?” His head moved to the side as he inspected her. “What’s your name, child?”

Gen’s spine straightened, and David took her hand, squeezing it gently in warning. He couldn’t put his finger on it, but he had the suspicion of magic and age. Deep and powerful.

“My name is Genevieve. Genevieve Fernly.”

The man turned to Vivienne. “You didn’t give her your name?”

Vivienne blanched. “I would have, but Luca refused that. She chose my father’s name instead when she came of age.”

The man grunted. “Well, Genevieve, I am your father, and it’s time we talked.”

David watched Genevieve blink slowly. “And who might that be?” he asked.

The man glared at him. “Padraic O’Shaunessy. Magician and—”

“Leprechaun?” David enquired.

The man’s eyes narrowed. “And what would you be knowing of them, laddie?”

David refused to be cowed by Padraic’s presence or the way he loomed over him.

“More than you’d imagine, Mr O’Shaunessy. I’m also Genevieve’s fiancé, so whatever you have to say to her, you also have to say to me.”

“Is that so?” Padraic muttered.

Genevieve’s eyes flashed. “Yes.”

Padraic sneered at David. “And what would it be that gave it away?”

David dragged Gen into his side. “It just clicked. You own the gold Eliminar outside. The expensive watch on your wrist is gold, I assume. Around your neck you wear a coin, the same as Gen’s. Also gold. The belt you wear, the buckle would also be gold, I’m guessing. The Irish in your voice. I could go on.”

“Clever man, for a human.”

David smiled. “Not so much these days.”

Padraic's eyes narrowed. "No?"

"Mr O'Shaunessy, I don't understand—" Gen's words were cut off.

"Pop. You call me Pop, Genevieve," Padraic responded.

"No. You're not the father I knew growing up. You weren't around for—"

"*I didn't even know about you.*" The words lashed like a whip, cutting through her furious refusal. "Not until this morning. Your mother came to see you, and I felt the tug of the coin I'd left with her. The magic in it, it stays with a person, and she wore it for many years. Until now."

David wanted to know why now but wisely kept himself quiet. These were questions he'd ask later.

"So, why are you here? Why now?"

The muscles in Padraic's face tightened. "The coin. Strong emotions power it. My connection to it, and through that to you, called. Summoned. Whatever term you want to use. I had to follow it. So yesterday, I called up my jet, and here I am." He flung out his hands. "But we should sit."

Gen kept a death grip on David's hand, and he didn't pull away, taking the seat beside her. "So, you came here for what?"

"That's the rub, young fellow. It called me, and I can't ignore that pull. Genevieve, your mother was supposed to let me know when and if something eventuated. But the coin didn't pull me back." Padraic whipped around so he could face the silent Vivienne.

"I didn't wear it. I wouldn't. You were a one-night event, dear." Her eyes gleamed. "I already had a mate. A powerful man, and I didn't know until she reached puberty. None of us did. By then, wearing it wasn't even a thought in my mind."

Padraic's eyes clouded, and David could see a looming battle. "So, you've just learned of Gen. What do you want now?" David asked.

"She must come back to Ireland with me. Take up her place in my world. My daughter is—"

"No way." Gen pushed out of her chair and shot up. "I don't care who you are. What you are. I'm happy in my life."

She stalked from the restaurant.

Padraic turned to David. “You must convince her, laddie. It’s in her best interests.”

“She’s a grown woman.”

“She’s only half of what she could and should be—"

“Somehow, I don’t think she cares,” David countered. “She’s made herself into a woman to be proud of.” He made to rise and follow Gen when Padraic snarled.

“You’ve got no idea. She’s a shifter, true. But she’s also a leprechaun. Until she can control the urge of the gold, it will tighten itself around her like a noose. To control it, and the magic she carries, she must learn of the lore.”

David’s knowledge of the old magics wasn’t strong, but the passion in Padraic’s voice had him stopping. “Give me your details. I won’t make any promises, but I’ll talk to her. It’s Gen’s decision at the end of the day.”

Padraic drew a card from a gold case and shoved it into David’s hand. “Persuade her. Work hard. Otherwise she’ll go mad from the hunger. I’ve seen it happen, and it’s not pretty.”

David glanced down at the card, unsurprised to see the raised gold printing. He rubbed a finger over the letters, then gave Padraic a short terse nod before turning and heading through the door to Gen.

CHAPTER 22

Genevieve couldn't accept that a man would claim her as his daughter after ignoring her presence for almost thirty years. "So, he just waltzes in, tells me I'm his daughter, and I'll have to go with him?" she seethed. "Fuck that! Fuck my mother too, because she must have known. All this time."

Fury had her fists balling. Good thing she'd left when she had. Otherwise, she may have said or done something to be regretted at a later point.

The car door opened, and David climbed inside. "Gen? Are you okay?" The concern in his voice had tears pricking her eyes.

"I'm fine," she growled, but really, was she?

"We should go home. Get some sleep." His words reminded her that they'd been awake now for over twenty-four hours.

"Yes." She turned the key in the ignition and headed for her apartment.

He didn't say a word, simply accepted her decision. Her eyes itched, her head ached, and fear became a bubble in her chest the farther she travelled.

Before either of them could climb from the car once she'd parked in her designated area, she turned to the man beside her. "David? Does this change how you see me?"

The whispered words had his head turning towards her. "No. You're my Genevieve. The woman I love and intend to spend my life with. Does this add another facet? Yes. But you're you. Just because you're a policewoman isn't the only reason I love you." He reached out, cupped her cheek. "Just because you're sexy also isn't the only reason I adore you. It's who you are inside. We can change the title, but that doesn't change the woman you are deep down inside."

Genevieve wasn't used to feeling fragile. Hadn't allowed that emotion to overtake her since she'd left her mother. After all, if she had, it might have drowned her.

"I hate feeling at sea," she muttered.

David snickered. "I can see that."

They reached the front door, and she opened it. For the first time, it didn't really feel like home. The apartment was and had been her refuge. She remembered David's suggestion that they should find somewhere else. Something bigger for the two of them.

"When we wake up, perhaps we might look online at some properties. Maybe make a short list?"

He stilled behind her, his hands settling on her shoulders. "You sure? We don't have to rush—"

"It's time, David. Time for me to show my commitment towards you." She turned and rose on her toes. Kissed him softly. "You're my future."

He hugged her against him, and she felt the beat of his heart. The way it beat to the same time as hers. "My yesterdays are gone, and my tomorrows are all yours, Genevieve."

She laughed. "That sounds like a wedding vow."

He blinked slowly. "I guess it does. Remind me to include that in the ceremony."

Love. It had certainly changed her outlook on life. "Come on, we should get some sleep."

"Especially if we're going to start house-hunting later."

They headed for the bedroom and found the clothes they'd left behind. His, a small bag of necessities including some toiletries, fresh clothes, and a pair of cotton pyjama bottoms.

Her eyebrows rose as he dressed in them. “Pyjamas?”

“So we sleep,” he answered.

“Ah. Okay.” She grinned and opened her drawers, pulling out a floaty chiffon baby doll.

“You’re killing me, Gen,” he groaned once she had it on. The blush colour left very little to the imagination, as did the ruffles and bows.

She sighed and sank to the bed, and when David pulled her into his embrace, the tension she’d tried hard to ignore felt as if it melted away.

“I love you, David.”

“And I love you too, Gen. Now sleep.”

It didn’t take long to release her grip on awareness.

Night fell quickly. While he dressed, Gen rang the lieutenant, who already seemed aware they wouldn’t be into the precinct that night.

“Tomorrow, we have to catch up on the vamp servant killers,” David muttered, and Gen nodded in agreement.

They travelled back to Cressida’s house in time to see the sun drop below the horizon.

“This is my last official task as a *Yeux Secondes* of the house,” he told Gen.

“They’ve found someone to replace you?”

“Yes. She’ll take over tomorrow. I’ll consult for a short while, but tonight, when we leave here, we should head back to the house. I need to pack my clothes. The rest of my effects are in storage,” David explained. “The set-up here was different. While I was at Xavier’s nest, I had an apartment. Furniture and so on.”

Gen wrinkled her nose.

“What?”

“Well, you chose all that with Alexa, right?”

David nodded. “Sure.”

“I hate to suggest it, but… maybe we should just get rid of it and start again. Without her ghosts hanging around." She bit her lip and glanced away.

Considering her suggestion, he could see how using the same things he and Alexa might be starting out on a tainted footing. Besides, he'd never really been a fan of the white furnishings she'd chosen. There were only a few pieces that he'd kept from his grandparents' time. Those were more important. "We should go through them, then. Once we settle on our property."

They'd spent time since waking looking through listings, but one house stood out for both of them, and they'd arranged to inspect it tomorrow.

"So, what's going to happen now?"

He gazed at Gen. So strong and taking all this upheaval in stride. Pride filled him, knowing she'd fully committed herself to him.

"I don't know. Cressida said to meet in the courtyard." And there they waited as the others drifted in.

In the courtyard, milling among the flowers, were the others from their now close-knit group. Xavier and Hope, Javed and Celina, together with Marian, Lucy, and Rachel.

David remembered the discussion he'd had with Daniel before he'd assumed the role of *Yeux Secondes* for Javed's nest: "Everyone is much happier now. We're a little less correct and upright."

"So? Now we're here, it's time to make some announcements," Hope called with a ready grin.

"We already know most of it." Javed had also unbent enough to show his cheeky side.

"Not everything." David strode forwards, towing his partner into the circle. "Tonight, I announce Genevieve has agreed to marry me."

A round of kisses and hugs, back slapping, and congratulations flowed.

Lucy stepped forwards. "Since everyone is making announcements, I guess we should share what we plan to do."

The girls looked among themselves and nodded. "You do it, Lucy. You're better at this." Rachel gripped Marian's hands as they waited.

"Well, okay. See, we've been talking. Now that we remember who and what we are, we have a choice. We can either look for any of our families or stay with Javed and Celina. We've talked a lot about our options."

Lucy took Celina's hand. "We want to stay. Celina and Javed. You're our parents now. You love us, care for us, and we just..." She stopped and gulped loudly.

"Unless you send us away, you're stuck with us is what Lucy is trying to say." Rachel spoke quietly, though her words carried deep emotions.

As one, they flung their arms around the couple and held on tight.

Now there were very few with dry eyes in the gathering.

From the gloom emerged three women. Their iridescent gowns shone by the light of the torches, and their hair was gathered up in elaborate sweeps. "Good, we're just in time."

"You!" Cressida stepped forwards, then, as if she'd hit a wall, stopped, eyes wide open.

"Cressida, forgive us for not telling all previously. You see, we couldn't. It wasn't our place." Selena spoke quietly, and Daniel saw more than one frown on the faces of those gathered.

Marian raised her head from Celina's skirts. "They can't. They're the Graces, and they can only help to resolve matters, not give the full answers."

"And how do you know that?" Daniel's voice cut through the surprise.

"The young one speaks true. She's touched, you know. Maybe one day, she too might be a Grace, if she chooses. But for now, she is a child. Bright and clever with the knack of seeing." Selena spread her arm out to the side. "But now, we have come to say our goodbyes. Our task here is complete, and we wish and long for rest. And home."

The other two witches nodded.

"What? You plan to leave?"

The three witches gave tired grins.

"Oh, we'll leave soon enough. But first we wish to grant you all something special. If any among you wish to be freed of the curse of the vampire..."

"What?" Hope squeaked the word, which echoed.

Daniel watched as gazes met and clung. Hope and Xavier were the first to shake their heads.

"For all there have been secrets passed in the blood, I wouldn't change who and what I am now." Hope grinned.

"Nor would I. It brought me Hope and friendships that will last for eternity." Xavier squeezed her hand.

Celina grinned. "I have my family and Javed. I don't need to change anything else."

Javed's arm still encircled Celina, but he tugged her a little closer. "And I've learned of real love, friendship, and family."

Cressida smiled. "I too have a family and a love I couldn't ever relinquish. Not even to death. Daniel?"

Daniel smiled. "And I will love my Cressida forever. Together with Samantha, we truly have everything we could ever ask for."

David coughed, and all gazes settled on him. "Well, Genny and I... she has so many things hidden from her. Secrets. She's my one. I know that, unlike before with Alexa. We've been talking... We want children in the future. We've only just found each other and need time to build what we have, but... I want her to know what is hidden from her."

Genny gripped his hands. "David?"

"Think of this as my gift to you, my love." He kissed her cheek tenderly.

"Perhaps, David, it's something you can both explore when you're ready." Cressida reached out and squeezed his hand.

The Graces turned to Genny, and Jemima reached out her hand, the welling of power tangible. "Well, then, when you're ready my dear, the answers shall become apparent. And with that, we bid you farewell." The witches rose and gifted the assembled vampires and humans with hugs.

Hand in hand, the three witches walked into the night without looking back.

"I don't think we'll see them again," Cressida said quietly, then turned back to the family.

"I'm not sure what you think is hidden, David," Gen whispered in his ear.

"I have no idea, but it's something your... Padraic said. But I won't push you, love. When you're ready I know how to contact him," he whispered back.

The group broke up shortly after, and he and Genevieve headed back to the nest, packing his clothes and loading them into the car.

He didn't stop for goodbyes, as was the way of nestlings. They would see each other again soon.

Once at Genevieve's house, they unloaded the boxes and hung clothes as she indicated in the closets and drawers. Only enough until they could decide on a property and move.

Contentment filled him. This was the first day of his new life, and the future before him, while hard and long, filled him with pleasure.

Gen had just settled down to her desk when the boss appeared. "You've got messages." He dumped the slips of paper on her desk. "Simon Bellingham, hmm?"

She scooped up the notations. "I don't know him. I mean, David does, so maybe it's for him."

"Perhaps, but the Lord of Lycans ringing you? Better return that call. Oh, and your ex-lover-boy, Julien? He's back."

There was antagonism and fury at the centre of the boss's words. "What's he doing back here?"

"Supposedly clearing out his desk, but he left something for you." He slid a large black box onto her desk.

Her hand hovered over the glossy cardboard. "I don't..."

"You should open it," the boss urged.

Genny's hands shook because something about this box felt wrong. Was it intuition? Some kind of magic?

She opened the box. Photos greeted her eyes, and below them...

"What the fuck?"

She pulled her hands away from the box, staring at what lay below. Purses, open to reveal the identities of their owners.

The missing women they were investigating the disappearances of.

She glanced to the boss, then slid open a drawer to her desk and tugged a pair of gloves free, drawing them on over her skin. She lifted each image and purse out, carefully inspecting and then repacking them into the box. At the bottom lay a letter.

A wave of emotion washed over her as she lifted and unfolded the sheet of paper.

Genevieve, ma coeur.

I never meant to keep these things, but you know shifters and our need to keep trophies. Like your mother and that coin. Yes, I know about it and your father. Such a shame that you will lose everything because she had to have a one-night stand.

I would have taken you away from all that confusing human trash. I planned to make you mine, then fight for control of the pack. Then you chose him, and my plans came to naught.

So, I guess this is your mess to clean up.

Me, well, I'm leaving town. Going to find somewhere to howl and enjoy the spoils of hunting. Somewhere far, far away. Now you can chase me. You can try, but dearest, you don't have the nose for this kind of hunt. I'd tell you to give it all up, but you won't.

I'm counting on that.

By the way, your new man may be a shifter, but he has no training. No knowledge of the magic and wonder we can instil. He'll never survive in a pack because you're an abomination against my kind. You should give him up now, before it's too late and he crosses some line and must face the trials. Because he simply won't survive.

Ah well. Your choice.

I won't bid you goodbye, simply adieu.

Julien

Her hands shook. "No. I won't let that happen." She reached for the piece of paper the boss had handed to her, aware he watched in silence.

For a moment, she wondered about the sanity of staying the course. Was she doing the right thing? In her heart, she knew the truth. She and David were meant to be. Nothing anyone said could change that for her. Whether it was the right decision, she'd agreed to a relationship and had no regrets. That one decision made her whole.

Love. Such a small word with the strongest and most powerful ties. It gave her hope. It filled the empty parts of her soul.

She dialled, her hands shaking. “Genevieve Fernly for Simon Bellingham,” she muttered once the call was answered.

Simon Bellingham joined her quickly on the line.

“I need your help, Lord of Lycans,” she blurted “Can you meet me?”

Did you enjoy this book by Imogene Nix?
There's more on the following pages. Just keep turning to see what else.

THE CELTIC CUPID TRILOGY

When Cupid—otherwise known as Diocail— is banished from his home on a remote Scottish Island, he's set a series of tasks by the great god Lugh, who also happens to be his father.

In ***Blame The Wine***, he must bring two lovers together... BBW Cara and James, the man she's lusted over from afar who happens to be a super geek and head Veha Industries.

In ***A Stranger's Embrace***, Diocail is driven to help an emotionally fragile Jane and Davis, a famous author. The task is more complicated, with the existence of Carstairs her could-be ex-husband and teenage daughter, Frannie.

In ***Revenge on Cupid***, Diocail must take the ultimate chance and find his own happily ever after with Simone. Sometimes the past gets in the way and HEA's don't come cheap though.

The dusty, dingy little diner was full, even with its current state of cleanliness—or lack thereof. People from the surrounding offices didn't care about anything except the incredible, well-prepared food at a reasonable cost. They flooded in, like waves to the shore. As one tide left, another swept in.

"Honestly, Simone. I'm going to try getting his attention one more time. If that doesn't work, I'm out of there. I mean, how long can I keep trying?" Cara picked at the caramel tart she hadn't been able to resist with the cheap metal fork and flicked the blob of fresh cream that sat on top to the side of the plate.

"You've said that tons of times before. Besides, what are you going to do to get his attention? Hmm? Walk naked through the typing pool?" Simone bobbed the straw in her smoothie as she eyed her friend with a frown. "It's been what? Eighteen months since you saw him, and you've mooned over him from a distance ever since you met him. You need to move on, Cara. That is, unless there's something you haven't shared?"

The query was arch. Cara shivered even as she shook her head. "No."

Simone quirked an eyebrow, obviously unconvinced with the answer. Cara let out a deep sigh of frustration. "There's a position…it's only temporary, for a PA reporting directly to him." She speared a forkful of tart, chewed quickly and swallowed, before continuing. "In his office, full-time for the period of the engagement. I saw the memo yesterday. I mean, I have the skills, right? I can type, answer phones, make coffee, file, greet people. What's more, I can probably do it better than all those size eights in the typing pool that Ms. Jackman seems to prefer." She nodded thoughtfully. "All I have to do is get past the ogre in Human Resources."

Simone stared at her, disbelief clear on her face. "Girl, I so remember that woman. If you think you can get past her, you're doing better than I ever did. That's why I left Veha Industries, remember? Maybe it's time to haul out your resumé and consider some other options. Look for something better." Simone shook her head and billows of her crimson hair swirled through the still air.

Cara understood Simone only had her best interests at heart. But this time she knew the outcome would be different. Hell, she could feel it in the air. The tingle of expectation.

"Cara, the HR ogre will hang you out for breakfast before she offers you anything like a position in that office. Remember her mantra? Good looks and good work make for a positive workplace!"

Simone didn't sugar-coat anything. It was another great reason for their long- term friendship. Honesty. But Cara didn't want to hear the truth in the statement. Even if it was exactly as her friend said.

Cara nodded quickly. "Yeah, I know, but if I don't try, then I won't know how close I can get to him, right? And the only way to catch his attention is to get past *her* and see him in person." Cara quaked a little at the information she needed to share. The favor she needed to ask. "Anyway, I tidied up my resumé and dropped the application into a memo envelope yesterday, so it's too late to back out now. I mean, fortune favors the brave. Doesn't it? If I don't snag an interview, I'm going to visit the career advisor across the street and register with them." She shrugged. "I'll look for temp work until something more long-term shows up. I can see what they have on offer and well...who knows? Maybe a job with the right boss is just waiting for me. But I'd rather this worked out, to be honest." Her voice trailed off into a whisper. "I really wish he would notice me."

Simone took a long slurp of her banana drink, and Cara noticed her questioning gaze even as she squirmed. Finally, Simone nodded. "It's your funeral. So anyway, you'd better show me this memo if you want me to be a referee for you. I'm guessing that's what you need, right? I'll have to know what I'm supposed to say about you before they ring."

Cara smiled. "Thanks, Simone. I knew I could count on you." She slipped a piece of paper out of her handbag and handed it over. "Sorry it's a bit creased. It was in the bottom of my bag, I stashed it so none of the others from the pool would see. You know how it is."

STAR OF ISHTAR

Warriors of the Elector
Book One

The first time Elara laid eyes on Grayson was when he rescued her from the clutches of a madman and his scientists who were kidnapping humans and conducting horrific experiments on them. That was years ago. In spite of her attempts to deepen their relationship, they remained nothing more than close friends.Now Elara is a medic with the Admiralty, and she knows what she wants. It's been Grayson since the beginning. When Elara is stationed on the *Star of Ishtar*, she arrives with a plan to further her career. But this time her plan has an added bonus—to finally get her man.

Grayson's spent years fighting the connection between himself and Elara. He's certain it only exist because he saved her life. But his will is failing, and he fears he just might give in to temptation.

"I finally made it." Elara Sudonne watched as the hull of the *Star of Ishtar* loomed in the inky darkness. She clutched her hands tightly together as the shuttle approached the hulking battleship.

This would be her new home and first combat ST placement for the Earth Empire. She quaked inwardly with nerves but fought to keep her serene exterior. Previously her deployments had consisted solely of on-planet expeditions and in rehabilitation and dirtside facilities. When the chance had arisen to move to the battleship, she'd grabbed it with both hands.

The frigid air chilled her bones as she sat in her shuttle seat, but a trickle of sweat inched its way down her back under the fresh gray wool flight uniform. Little puffs of vapor escaped her mouth as she rubbed her arms. Nerves stretched tight, she looked through the small portal at the front of the vessel. She wanted to tug at the collar that somehow seemed to have grown tighter as the ship loomed ahead, but instead she firmed her mouth, straightened her spine, and concentrated on the future.

"So damned long." She'd been working toward this outcome since the day Grayson Myatt and Duvall McCord had saved her from her Ru'Edan captors. She was lucky, she'd survived the 'experimentation' of the Ru'Edan leader Crick Sur Banden's scientists. "And all I have to remind me are my scars." She didn't grin at her own joke.

The person seated behind her jostled but she ignored it, lost in her memories. On that day, so very long ago, the young Elara, fresh-faced and with idealistic views of the empire, was taken from the mall where she'd been shopping with friends, thrust into the back of a transport vehicle, and given to the Ru'Edan scientists to experiment on.

For days they'd worked on her and others, seeking an average pain threshold of humans, slicing her skin then noting reactions and how long it took to heal. They'd cut her arms, body, and even her face, and now she carried the extensive scarring of the exercise as a reminder to herself and others of what they were fighting for. Freedom. The freedom of Earth and its allied planets.

She'd never relinquished hope, it had been her constant companion as she fought against the all-consuming terror. Then they'd found her in that dirty, disused warehouse. They'd found others too, in various states of death and decay. The smells of despair had filled the air with a fetid ripeness that she'd never been able to forget.

Since that day she'd promised herself that she would pay the Ru'Edan back for what they'd done to her. What they'd taken from her. Over the years, she tempered and honed the rage while remaining adamant that she would see the final act played out. She couldn't physically fight, but she had learned about trauma, knew it and understood how it affected a person, and used it as a weapon.

The iron will forged through her experiences had fed her determination, and she'd applied herself to study, finishing in the top ten percent of her class. She entered the medical program at the academy, working hard to excel. Her family remained supportive if perplexed as to why she had chosen to keep reminding herself of what had happened.

The maw of the *Star of Ishtar* loomed closer, opening its cavernous mouth as she watched through the portal. She could hear the voices of the shuttle crew signaling their intention to enter and land, the tinny confirmation coming swiftly. She watched avidly while the shuttle maneuvered, imagining the invisible shields dropping to allow it entry.

Her hands twisted with fear and anger, but she tamped down her emotions. Anger never helped anyone. Staying strong, knowing your history, and ensuring it couldn't be repeated, they were the answers, she told herself firmly, pulling herself from the grip of a dark past so horrific she still saw it in her dreams. She pushed it away to the recesses of her mind and focused on what she was about to do.

A squark overhead, the usual mechanical sound that alerted all on board to a transmission by the captain, caught her attention. "Attention all passengers. We are entering the shuttle bay. Please ensure when you disembark you remove all personal items. Move beyond the white line and wait for your designation."

The lights of the bay flashed as they entered, and once again Elara marveled at how far humanity had moved since they had first walked the Earth. She saw the opening of the structure as the shuttle moved into the bay, inching forward slowly until it stopped its ponderous motion and began its descent to the floor. Something deep inside warmed even as the shuttle's environmental systems began to synchronize with the cooler temperature of the *Star of Ishtar*, and she felt a smile crawl its way over her face.

Elara breathed in deeply, inhaling the metallic-tasting, recycled air and welcoming the calmness that settled on her body. Her eyes closed as she filled her lungs. "I'm here." There was more than a little satisfaction in her tone, and she smiled. She slowly exhaled, finding that center of peace she relied on.

A loud thud and clank echoed as the deep drone split the air. The engines were powering down, and there she was, on one of the Earth Empire's Emeritus class battleships. She sat in her seat, waiting for the all clear from the captain, and once it sounded through the cabin, she rose, tugging at the webbing belt and disengaging it.

The small backpack beside her was all she carried as she made her way to the exit, not needing to duck as so many others did. She stepped through the door, her hands gripping the rail of the cold, metal stairs which connected to the side of the gray shuttle.

She clambered down them slowly, savoring the experience. The sting of the cold on her hands from the stairs, frigid from even their brief exposure to the blackness of space, made her flinch inwardly. The shuttle journey from the Admiralty's strategic base at Aenna to their current position had taken just over an hour, but the whole time it felt like her heart had been in her throat. Her mouth was dry as she followed the new recruits from the ship into the landing bay. She stopped, silently noting the slight mustiness of the air, the recycled quality easily recognizable. Everything, including the oxygen, needed recycling in space.

All around her people swarmed, either around the ships or into the dogleg line that now formed ahead of her. Someone had opened the baggage locker of the shuttle, and the sound of dropping bags hitting the plascrete floor echoed in the air. Another crewmember guided trolleys to the other side of the shuttle, pulling out boxes with important day-to-day items for the ship, including vaccines and plants. She watched briefly, all the while listening to the alien cacophony. Voices called in welcome to old crewmembers, while new ones watched, many goggle-eyed in the fresh uniforms of newly minted officers and crewmembers.

Her gaze flicked around quickly, taking in the sights, sounds, and smells, pungent with oils and grease; burning smells from the scorched plascrete and the press of sweaty or nervous bodies. She joined the line silently, tacking onto the end, and stayed at parade rest, knowing the welcoming voice would cut through the air soon enough. She felt somehow disconnected from the main throng. Perhaps the knowledge that this was the outcome she had worked for years to achieve set her apart. However, still, she felt so...distant from everything around her. She smiled secretly at the bout of whimsy.

"Attention!" The voice boomed out over the plascrete of the docking bay, and she snapped her body into position, noting the commander who had bellowed the words. Technically, she outranked most members aboard the *Star of Ishtar*, except for the command and leadership staff, but she knew all newcomers had to join the welcoming parade, regardless of rank.

Fleet Captain Elphin came into view, his tired features topped by salt-and-pepper gray hair, which highlighted his cool blue eyes. Elara also recognized a body prone to a little middle-aged thickness. Following behind him was his second-in-command, Duvall McCord. A young up-and-coming officer, his status as a fast-tracking officer heading toward his own command, with Elphin both his mentor and captain, had become almost legendary at the academy.

She looked closely at McCord, noting the dynamic drive of his actions and movements. Soon he would achieve a promotion to captain, and she rejoiced for her friend. She'd followed his career with interest and had to tamp down a smile as his eyes betrayed the shock of seeing her before settling into their flat command persona. So he hadn't been apprised of her deployment, she noted, and she had to restrain the tiny feeling of surprise and satisfaction. She filed that snippet of information away.

She caught sight of the man standing behind Duvall. Grayson Myatt. He'd made her heart beat faster for years. Tall and blond with a muscular build and a sexy, tight, little butt, he had pools of deep-blue eyes that had always made her think of forever. He had a growth of stubble on his chiseled jaw, and her fingers itched to touch his perfect lips. Yes, since the day he'd found her in that nasty warehouse tied down like a ragged animal, she'd worshipped him from afar.

Now she had her opportunity to tangle with him, hopefully much closer than any chance that had ever come her way before. With a sigh, she pulled her gaze back to the captain and forced herself to concentrate on his words. She couldn't afford to have her commanding officer angry due to her being distracted.

"Welcome to the *Star of Ishtar*. Most academy recruits want to join us because of what we represent, but on this ship, we only take the best of the best. So, if you made it here, you're the ones we wanted to take a look at. Getting here is only the first step. Staying here is harder to achieve. Our people are the best. Earn your place, and in return, we'll make you one of our crew—a member of the *Star of Ishtar*. Only the best and the brightest wear our uniform and badge. You'll be expected to perform to your absolute limit then give some more. We don't tolerate people who don't pull their weight. Do us proud and wear your uniform with pride." The captain looked out over the new members of his crew. His voice had echoed during his speech, and now it died away.

He scanned the faces before him, and she could almost read his thoughts. There were new security officers and a smattering of other crew. Some of them were young and impressionable, and she knew a few wouldn't make the cut as crewmembers. Others would carve out their place on the *Star of Ishtar* and move to better positions and placements, like she would: the new SurgiTech, a younger female, experienced but untried on board a ship. She smiled at that thought.

Some of those who stood with her would be replaced as they failed the exacting standards the captain set. She'd heard that he was a firm captain, fair but demanding. He'd have to be to command this ship. The Ishtar had well over five hundred at full capacity, and the captain could select their placements as his command staff saw fit from the many who applied to join the crew. She sensed his satisfaction with the choices in the relaxation of his body.

Abruptly, he turned to Duvall, breaking her study of him. "Get them to where they need to present themselves." His words echoed as he walked away. He had a purposeful stride. Quick but unhurried, like he knew where he was going and how to get there. A man who knew how to get what he wanted. Someone to respect and admire.

"My name is Commander Duvall McCord. I am your second-in-command, and my direct subordinate is Commander Grayson Myatt. While you are aboard the *Star of Ishtar* you will be required to fulfill your duties efficiently. As Captain Elphin said, do your job right and you will be one of ours, with all the benefits that come with being a crewmember of the *Star of Ishtar*."

He paused and eyeballed each of the newer recruits, those fresh from the academy. Many of them paled under his gaze, and she smiled inwardly. Even the older people in the line seemed to quake beneath his scowl. He'd always had that air of innate authority, even when barely out of the academy himself. She knew his methods and watched him make full use of the carefully practiced tone of presence.

"Each of you has been assigned. You will present yourselves to the chief of your section. Those details will be found in your orders. Commander Myatt has organized a team to escort you to your cabins. You will have approximately one hour to prepare. We've arranged for crewmembers to escort you to your superiors. Be ready to present for duty. Any issues, you will, of course, take up with your section commander. Should there be need to take any further action, you will see Commander Myatt. You should only see me if you are a command crewmember or as a point of discipline. I am not one for small talk, so if you present to me, have a very good reason."

He delivered the words slowly and deliberately, and Elara restrained a small smile on hearing at least one gulp from those in the line nearest her.

"We run a tight ship here. Discipline and commitment are the two key factors we look for beyond loyalty in our crew. You will from henceforth represent our ship everywhere, and we do not tolerate anything less than the best." He looked around once more, the stern demeanor he wore so well reinforcing the message. If she hadn't known him for so long, she too might have missed the hint of humor glinting in his eyes, the one many took for coldness.

Her legs ached, and she wanted to move and relieve the pressure on them, but she held herself still, waiting for the command to dismiss. She wouldn't let herself or him down now. Not after she'd worked so long to achieve this position.

As the new ST, she had no previous experience on ships. She had vast experience in the field, but Elara was aware that would count for little in the eyes of most of the crew. She didn't intend to signal a weakness to anyone and least of all on her first day aboard the *Star of Ishtar*. That thought held her still and controlled.

She had big shoes to fill after her predecessor, Jamieson, had retired, even though she knew she could fill the void he'd left behind. As a long-term member of the crew—over twenty years—his tenure on the *Star of Ishtar* had placed him aboard since its launch. Due to his experience in the heat of battle with the Ru'Edan he had made a name for himself as the coldest of cold in the hottest of situations. She hoped to emulate that herself and carve out her own place aboard the Ishtar, as its crew lovingly knew her.

Duvall and Grayson knew how much she wanted to prove herself. They just wouldn't have expected it here, on the Ishtar.

She watched Duvall study her, then, quickly turning on his heel, call to those assembled, "Dismissed."

Once they started to move away, she softened her stance, preparing to turn when the call came.

"Sudonne! A moment if you please."

Elara turned to face Duvall. "Commander?"

"Welcome to the *Star of Ishtar*, Elara. While I am surprised you're the new ST, Grayson and I are pleased you could join us. But how did you manage to pull it off? Keeping it quiet that you were the new ST?" he asked, his voice deep enough to make most women shiver with anticipation.

She smiled, thinking it was a shame she didn't have any feelings for him except sisterly attachment, but then again, given his lack of deep commitment to women, maybe it wasn't such a shame after all.

She understood what drove him. He wanted his own ship and to captain his own future. They'd spent many nights over wine or ale discussing his beliefs that commitment grounded a person. Inwardly, she shrugged. He'd make those calls for himself, though she was sure that one day he would come across someone who would make him consider his choices a little more thoroughly.

"I'm pleased to be here, Duvall. Having an uncle who happens to be an admiral, he was able to let Captain Elphin know that I wanted to surprise you. It's a small world in the Admiralty. Elphin already knew of me, so he okayed my placement. Once the powers knew there was no impediments to me joining the crew, it was fairly simple from there." She felt a small smile creep onto her face, then let it drop away. "What do you think Grayson thinks?"

"Ah, still chasing him, are you?" He grinned, his eyes twinkling. "I think he'll be pleased you're finally old enough and you're here." He looked her straight in the eye. "But you may just need to remind him of that particular fact." He motioned for her to go before him, barking out a deep laugh. "Come on, I'll show you to your cabin."

Available from Love Books Publishing
Available in Ebook via Books2Read

Direct Autographed Copy
https://www.imogenenix.net/Warriors1

THE BLOOD BRIDE BY IMOGENE NIX

Hope just wants to be an ordinary nestling. She went to college and escaped, but now she's back and there's a secret everyone is keeping from her.

Xavier is the new master of the nest, ready to welcome home the daughter of the house who he has never met. He's unprepared for the woman who steals his breath and enchants him.

Now Hope and Xavier must fight for lives and those of the innocents. After all, it is only by overcoming the rogues that they will have a chance of a timeless future together. But will it be in time?

PROLOGUE

As silence descended on the house, the shadows grew—dark grays and blacks that bled into each other. First one figure then another broke away, making a run toward the house. Silent as the grave, they moved swiftly over dew-slicked grass. Then they stopped still. Waiting. Not a movement betrayed them until a signal propelled them back into action and they started crawling upwards. The walls damp coating no barrier to the intruders that ascended in the darkness.

The sound of each window breaking shattered the quiet—the figures were inside. Screams echoed through the night. Yet, in this area of large estates, heavy with noise-absorbing shrubbery, no one could hear those within. The blood-curdling screams went on and on before finally dying away.

Just one sound echoed through the night: The sobbing of a child.

The front door opened and figures trooped out—ghostly specters against an inky night sky, broken by a single outline. A child in white, carried at the center of the pack.

No sound broke the silence as they moved toward the trees surrounded the house.

Flames now licked at the manor: A deathly glow of oily smoke rising.

All that remained was a single person—wrapped in a cape of midnight blue beyond the house—watching them melt away.

Jemima moved toward the burning structure, breaking into a run as she breached the threshold. Vainly she attempted to enter, but the heat drove her back.

Now dashing tears from her face, she raced across the graveled driveway toward the gates, where the guardhouse was located. No sign of life existed within the building and some instinct of survival slowed her pace to a careful creep. Out of breath and heaving from exertion, she nervously checked within.

Small puffs of white vapor colored the glass. She darted from one window to another. Her cloak drawn tightly around her body, hoping it would camouflage her from sight.

Satisfied, Jemima entered through the heavy, wooden front door and moved toward the phone she spied on the floor. Her eyes darting here and there she dialed, listening to the rotary motor as it returned to the proper position. Time was short and if *they* came back, she needed to have shared the message.

The phone rang once. Twice. With a brrping sound it connected.

"Hello?" A male answered and she felt a warm flush of relief at the voice. A voice she knew well.

"The manor has been breached. The girl child taken." The words erupted and her hand trembled.

"On our way." The click of the receiver being replaced echoed loudly in the stillness of the room.

Copper. She smelled copper.

Her stomach soured, knowing it meant more deaths. Jemima looked around for the gun—a gun with deadly, holy water-infused copper bullets—she knew was hidden somewhere in the room. A gun she couldn't find. *No divine intervention exists here*, she thought.

Hopefully *they* didn't remain. Feeding. If they were still here, that's what they would be doing. She found a corner and scrunched down, hiding from sight.

Crouched low, she tried to stay as still as possible, listening for sounds of the vehicles she knew would be coming. She dug her fingers into the flesh of her arms; remaining aware enough to stop before drawing blood. That would surely bring them out. Jemima dragged the cloak around her to capture the warmth, yet there was little to be found.

The sounds of engines roused her from the corner of the room. Jemima inched toward the window, the lead of the old glass distorting her view, hearing raised voices she knew Mistress Cressida had arrived.

Jemima retreated. Remained hidden from the woman because if

she knew, all may well be lost. From the shadowed room she listened to the conversation...

"It smells like Estersham." The Mistress' eyes closed. "If it is, we have a problem." She turned once more, her face set and eyes now glacial in intensity. "James?"

The man nodded as if he knew what was to come.

"If I take those steps, I cannot return. Another must stand in my place." Her voice hardened while her eyes glittered in the dim light, piercing in their intensity.

Then the Mistress' voice called out in the near silence. "You and yours have been my loyal servants for so many years. I took an oath to protect you long ago. I renewed it with marriage and births, over and over. Now, my home and yours have been breached and this child taken from us. The girl child, who will be the hope and salvation of our kind, was ripped from the bosom of our nest. I will repay your loyalty and I will get her back." The words of power rippled in the night and licked at Jemima's skin.

ALSO BY IMOGENE NIX

Warriors of the Elector

- Star of Ishtar
- Starline
- Starfire
- Star of the Fleet
- Starburst
- The Star of Eternity

The Star of Ishtar & Starline - Print

Starfire & Star of the Fleet - Print

Starburst & The Star of Eternity - Print

Blood Secrets

- The Blood Bride
- The Illuminated Witch
- The Sorcerer's Touch

House Secrets (The Blood Secrets Continuation)

- As Dawn Breaks (coming 2021)
- Immortal Consequences (coming 2021)

The Automaton Series

- Haven House (coming 2022)
- Nobel Crest (coming 2022)

The Search Duology

- Miss Elspeth's Desire

- Miss Isabelle's Craving

Reunion Trilogy

- War's End
- The Assassin
- Executing Justice

The Reunion Trilogy in Paperback

The Webs Series

- Fated Webs
- Tangled Webs
- Covert Webs

The Webs Series Paperback

21st Testing Protocol

- Cyborg: Redux
- Children Of A Greater Evil
- When Evil Came To Stay
- Finis: The War To End All Wars

Celtic Cupid Trilogy

- Blame The Wine
- A Stranger's Embrace
- Revenge On Cupid

The Celtic Cupid Trilogy in Paperback

Zombieology

- The Reset (2018 - Love At The End of The World)
- I Dream of Zombies
- The Six Million Dollar Zombie
- Make Room For Zombies (Coming 2022)

Knights of Pleasure

- Silken Knights (Not Yet Released)

Single Titles

The Chocolate Affair (also in Print)

Falling In Love Again (Previously A Sapphire For Karina)

BioCybe (also in Print)

Hesparia's Tears (also in Print)

Tomorrow's Promise

A Bar In Paris (also in Print)

Inheritance Of The Blood (also in Print)

The Plan

Loving Memories (also in Print)

Hero of Heartbreak Hill (also in Print)

My One & Only

Curse Bound (coming 2021)

Raspberry Dreams (Not Yet Released)

Non Fiction

Self Publishing: Absolute Beginners Guide (With Suzi Love)

Written as Ciara Cave

25 Curated Ways To Get Rid Of Telemarketers

Book Signings for Absolute Beginners

ABOUT THE AUTHOR

Imogene is published in a range of romance genres including Paranormal, Science Fiction and Contemporary. She is mainly published in the UK and USA.

In 2010, Imogene Nix (the pen name not Imogene herself) was born. Imogene sat down and worked tirelessly for 3 months culminating in the book Starline, which became the first in a trilogy titled, "Warriors of the Elector." Since then she's had over 30 titles published and is now focusing on hybridising herself - with a mixture of traditionally published and self-published works.

In fact, she's taking control of many of her back catalogue books, which are slowly re-releasing as self-published titles.

Imogene is a member of a range of professional organisations world wide, and believes in the mantra of mentoring and paying it forward and is actively involved in mentorship (through NaNoWrimo and her vlog: In The Chair With Imogene Nix) and tutoring of new and upcoming authors.

In her spare time she loves to drink coffee, wine & eat chocolate and is parenting her spoiled dog and a ferocious cat along with her husband and 2 human daughters and looks forward to weekends away with her husband in their caravan "The Seven Year Hitch!" Do look forward to her caravan romance at some point!

To Contact Imogene

www.imogenenix.net

imogene@imogenenix.net

facebook.com/ImogeneNix
twitter.com/ImogeneNix
instagram.com/ImogeneNix
bookbub.com/authors/imogenenix

www.ingramcontent.com/pod-product-compliance
Ingram Content Group UK Ltd.
Pitfield, Milton Keynes, MK11 3LW, UK
UKHW020143250726
13967UKWH00002B/833

9 781922 369284